More about BULGAKOV and MANDELSTAM

glas

NEW RUSSIAN WRITING

5

Editor:
Natasha Perova

UK editor: Dr. Arch Tait
US editor: Ed Hogan

Literary Consultants:
Sally Laird, Tom Birchenough, Jill Parry

Designed by Emma Ippolitova
Typeset by Tatiana Shaposhnikova

GLAS Publishers, Moscow 119517, P.O.Box 47, Russia

UK address for enquiries, subscriptions and payments:
GLAS, c/o Dept. of Russian Literature,
University of Birmingham, B15 2TT
Tel.: 021-414 6044, Fax: 021-414 5966

North America Sales and Editorial office, GLAS
c/o Zephyr Press, 13 Robinson Street, Somerville MA 02145
Tel: (617) 628-9726, Fax: (617) 776-8246

ISBN 5-7172-0003-X
ISBN US 0-939010-40-2

Издание этого номера осуществлено за счет средств русских и иностранных редакторов.

CONTENTS

Mikhail
BULGAKOV

/1891 – 1940/

Bulgakov's father. 1907.

Bulgakov's mother in mourning sitting under her husband's portrait.
Spring 1907.

Vera, Mikhail, Nadya and Varya Bulgakovs.1897.

Bulgakov, a student of Grammar School No.1 in Kiev.1908.

Bulgakov, 1909.

Bulgakov in 1910s, his university years.

Bulgakov in his room in No.13 Andreevsky Spusk, Kiev, 1913.

N.Nikitinsky, Bulgakov, Lydia Belozerskaya.
Bulgakov grew up in Kiev, a city of glaring contrasts in those days. It was also a city of great cultural traditions which the writer was exposed to at the Grammar School and the University,to say nothing of his family. And then there was the beauty of the city itself which brought a particular charm to the life there.

Bulgakov in 1926.

S.Toplenikov, Nikolay Lyamin, Lydia Belozerskaya, Bulgakov's second wife. "Everything about Bulgakov — spotlessly white collar and carefully knotted ties, the unfashionable but well-cut suit, the trousers with a knife-edge crease, his kissing of ladies' hands, and the almost haut-monde formality of his bow — everything about him set him apart from the rest of us." — Emily Mindlin, his colleague on Nakanune.

Bulgakov in the 1930s.

"Do remember me, my dear Seryozha. Yours, little loving Bulgakov. Moscow, 29 October 1935."

Bulgakov in the role of the Judge in Dickens' "The Pickwick Papers", 1934, the only role he played in the Moscow Art Theatre.

Villa Schönblick
Friedrichstr. 2
Badenweiler
Schwarzwald

Дорогой и милый
Михаил Афанасьевич
Вы не представляете себе до какой степени я рад Вашему вступлению в наш театр!
Мне пришлось поработать с Вами лишь на нескольких репетициях Турбиных и я тогда почувствовал в Вас – режиссера (а м.б. и артиста?!)
Мольер и многие другие совмещали эти профессии с литературой!
От всей души приветствую Вас искренно верю в успех и очень бы хотел поскорее поработать вместе с Вами
До скорого и приятного свидания.
Думаю вернуться в средине октября
Искренно Вам преданный
К. Станиславский
1930.
4/IX Баденвейлер

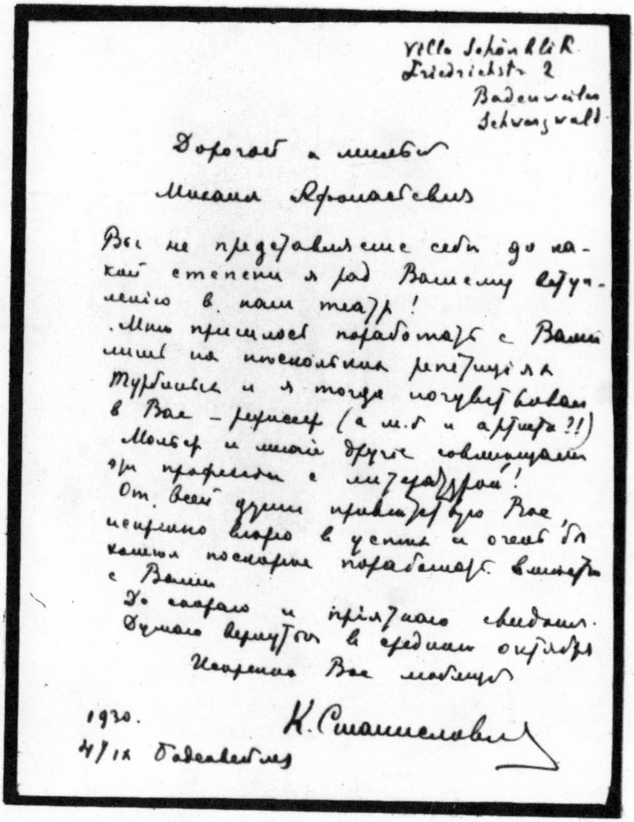

Stanislavsky's letter of greeting to Bulgakov.

"My dear Mikhail Afanasyevich,
there is no telling how happy I am that you are joining our theatre. I had a chance to work with you at the rehearsals of The Turbins. I immediately sensed a stage director in you (and perhaps an actor as well). Moliere and many others combined these professions with writing. I greet you from the bottom of my heart and sincerily believe in your success. I am looking forward to our working together and hope to see you soon. I'll probably be back in mid-October.

Yours sincerily

K. Stanislavsky

4.9.30"

Moscow Art Theatre.
He worshipped the theatre and hated it at the same time. He felt that Stanislavsky and Nemirovich betrayed him. He said that the theatre was "the cemetery of his plays".

Collage from the magazine "New Spectator" (1926) featuring Bulgakov's characters.

Bulgakov's study in his flat in Furmanov Street.

Bulgakov in 1936.

Bulgakov in the late 193Os

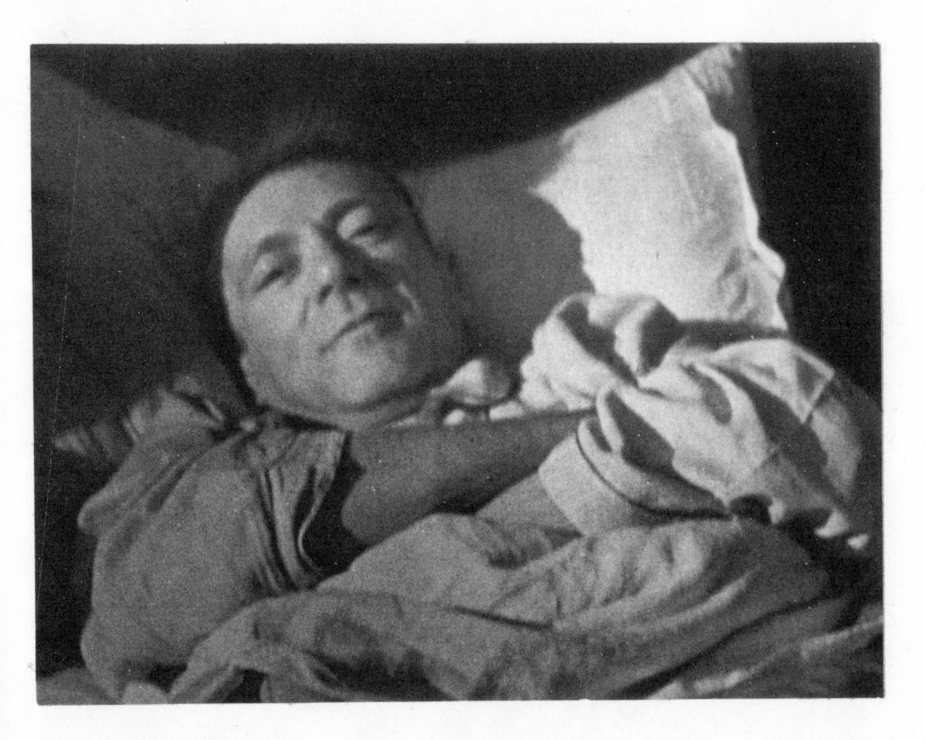

In the last year of his life.

Patriarch's Pond, the place of action in *The Master and Margarita*.

Here he lived in a communal flat.

MIKHAIL BULGAKOV, the son of a professor at the Kiev Theological Academy, was born on 3 May 1891. After leaving grammar school in 1909, he went on to study at Kiev University's Department of Medicine from which he graduated in 1916. In 1916-17 he worked as general practitioner in Smolensk Province and moved back to Kiev in 1918 where he worked in front-line hospitals. In 1921, he settled in Moscow which became his permanent home. Between 1921-24, he contributed short satirical pieces to the newspaper *Gudok* and the Germany-based *Nakanune*.

He had known the hopelessness of Russian provincial life, he had witnessed the bloody events of the Civil War in Kiev, took part in the fighting in the Caucasus, practiced as a venereologist and had been at various times an actor, an MC, a lecturer, a lexicographer and even an engineer. All of these along with his experience as a reporter imprinted themselves on his sensitive memory.

In 1924 the first part of *The White Guard* was printed in the *Rossia* magazine but it was closed down soon afterwards. In 1926, Bulgakov's most famous play, *The Days of the Turbins* (based on *The White Guard*) was staged at the Moscow Art Theatre while later, in 1930-36, Bulgakov worked as an assistant director there and even played the part of the Judge in Dickens's *The Pickwick Papers*. His other plays, however, incurred the wrath of the censors and had only very short runs. Although Bulgakov had something of a love-hate relationship with the Moscow Art Theatre it is known that Stanislavsky declared that the theatre would have to close down unless the ban on the Turbins was lifted.

Between the late 1920s and 1961 his books were not published in Russia at all and Bulgakov acquired the reputation of a "forgotten writer". But during the "thaw" the

"Bulgakov phenomenon" suddenly began its triumphant march across the world. Like a storm his fame surged, spreading from literary circles to a much wider readership.

His famous prophesy that "manuscripts do not burn" was to prove particularly true after his death.

Between 1921-25, Bulgakov kept a diary which was confiscated by the police, and although it was later returned to him he burnt it and never kept any notes from that day. (It was recently found in the KGB archives and published by *Ogonyok.*)

He was constantly castigated by critics for "distorting Soviet reality". He would pedantically cut out any reference to himself (as he later got his wife to do) and stick them in an album. These made a whole volume with hardly a good word in it, nothing but rude attacks on him or downright slander.

Bulgakov was earning nothing as an author and could not even count on a contract with a theatre or a publisher.

When all his plays were banned and he gave up hope of ever to be allowed to publish his books he applied for permission to emigrate. He wrote several letters to Stalin and after a long delay Stalin telephoned Bulgakov in response to his letter of March 28, 1930. During that short conversation Bulgakov was promised to be reinstated at the Moscow Art Theatre and he decided to stay in Russia.

The figure of Bulgakov, bloodied yet unbound, is of tremendous significance to us in human terms. He is an urban writer, laconic, a master of suspense. But there is another aspect to his style which merits comment too and that is his "Britishness". For here's an author whose attributes the British in particular can appreciate—proper reserve, a devastating sense of humour, respect for tradition and above all, in the face of adversity, a stiff upper lip.

Mikhail Bulgakov
To a Secret Friend

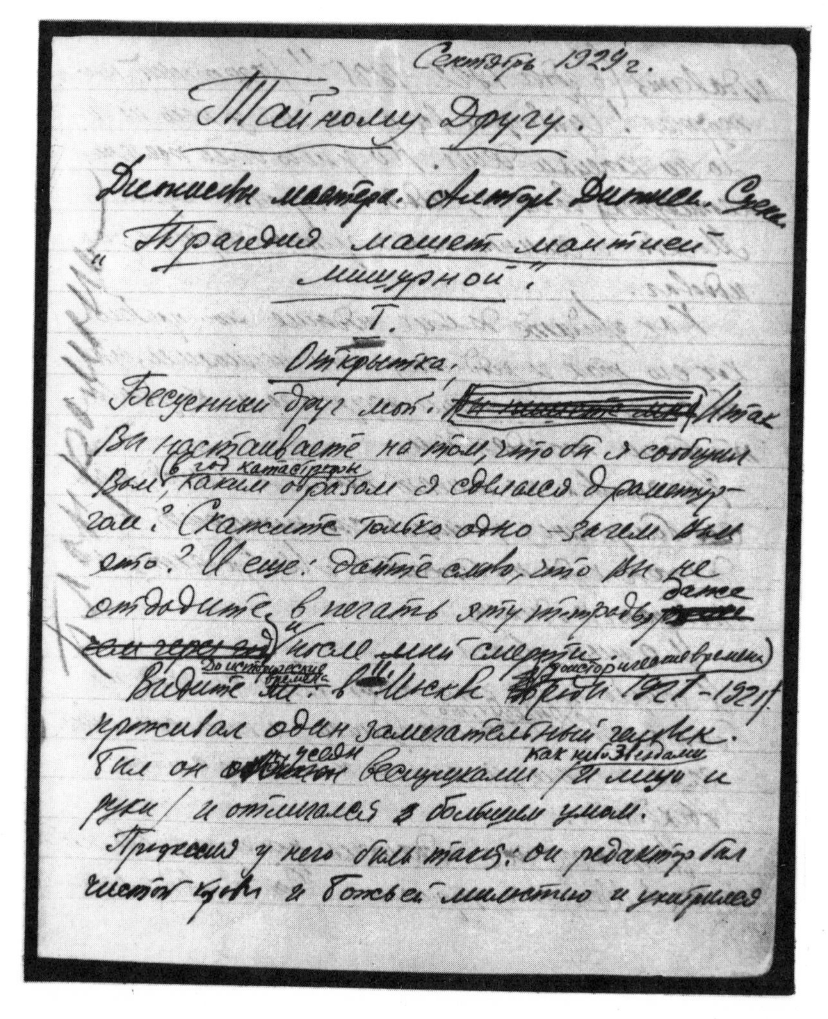
Сентябрь 1929 г.

Тайному другу.

"Трагедия машет мантией мишурной".

I.

Открытка.

Бесценный друг мой! Итак Вы настаиваете на том, чтобы я сообщил Вам в год катастрофы, каким образом я сделался драматургом? Скажите только одно — зачем Вам это? И еще: дайте слово, что Вы не отдадите в печать эту тетрадь даже и после моей смерти.

Видите ли: в Москве в 1921–1921 проживал один замечательный человек. Был он усеян веснушками как кирпичами (и лицо и руки) и отличался большим умом.

The first page of the manuscript "To a Secret Friend".

From 1922 to 1926, Bulgakov worked on the newspaper Gudok, first as a "processor" re-writing other authors' work, and then as a topical satirist. He also contributed to Nakanune, the Russian-language newspaper published in Germany between 1922-24. This newspaper had a branch office in Moscow and its Literary Supplement was edited by Alexei Tolstoy. According to the critic Lydia Yanovskaya, "To a Secret Friend" is the beginning of Bulgakov's Black Snow (Theatrical Novel), in fact an earlier version, dated September 1929. It is made up of autobiographical stories about the publication of his first novel (Notes on the Cuff) and his work on "a certain major newspaper", which we can recognise as Gudok. Although unfinished it reads as an independent work, full of Bulgakov's characteristic wit and lively interest in life. The manuscript has been lovingly preserved by Bulgakov's widow, Elena Sergeyevna, among other papers in her priceless archives.

1. POSTCARD

My precious friend! So you insist that in this year of catastrophe I inform you **how I became a playwright**? Just tell me one thing — why do you need to know? And also: promise you will never let this notebook be published even after my death.

II. PREHISTORIC TIMES

Well, now, in prehistoric times (the years 1921-1925) there was a splendid fellow who lived in Moscow. He was covered with freckles, like the sky with stars (both face and hands), and was exceptionally brainy.

As for his profession, he was a pure-bred editor by the grace of God and managed to publish (in the years 1922-1925) a good-sized journal! The most monstrous thing of all was that he didn't have a bean. But he did have an incredible iron will, and, sitting in a nice, dirty flat on the outskirts of the city of Moscow, he did his publishing.

As you will see later, this activity had remarkable consequences for both him and a number of other people whom inexorable fate had brought together under the auspices of this journal.

If a chap has no money, yet is devoured by an unhealthy imagination, he has to hurry off somewhere. And my editor hurried off to see someone.

And talked to him.

With the result that this someone took over the publishing. Paper appeared, from nowhere, and books, slim ones at first then fat ones, began to come out.

The publisher immediately went bust. And how! Good and proper. All that remained of him was a smoking hole.

You want to know why I'm telling you all this? How can I not tell you! You asked **how I became playwright**, so I'm telling you.

Yes. Well then, he went bust.

So bust that when fate cast me into the very house and flat where the bankrupt fellow had taken refuge, I saw what (in his opinion) was his only hope of salvation. It was the following. A large sheet of paper with water colour paintings of the leaders of the 1917 revolution, surrounded by a wreath of hammers, sickles and ears of corn. The sickles were painted mauve, the hammers black and the ears of corn yellow. The leaders looked dark, sad and most unlike themselves.

All this had been painted by the hand of the unfortunate bankrupt, who at that time was guilty of unauthorised expenditure to the tune of eighteen thousand roubles (you realise, of course, that his main business was not running a private journal) with debts of forty thousand to the state and thirteen thousand to private individuals.

Why?

He hoped, you see, that some publisher would purchase this work of art and print it in a vast number of copies, then every organisation in the land would buy it and hang it on their walls.

I never saw the poster anywhere, from which I conclude that no one did in fact buy it.

Actually, the author of the painting did not stay long in his room in Prechistenka Street. When it became empty except for one sofa, the unfortunate fellow took to his heels. Where did he go? I can't say. Perhaps at this very moment, as you are reading these lines, he is in Saratov or Rostov-on-Don, or, most likely, in Berlin. But wherever he is, I still won't get my thousand odd roubles.

So: the journal was at the printers, the unfortunate bankrupt in Buenos-Aires, the editor...

You are wondering where my editor made his money before he met the unfortunate bankrupt?

This mystery has now been solved, and it was I who guessed the answer. I can just see you laughing! If you were here with me, you would probably say that I couldn't have guessed. But I'm not really so hopelessly stupid, my friend, am I? Though you are cleverer than me, I agree... Anyway, I did guess the answer: he sold his soul to the Devil. And it was the son of perdition who supplied him with money. But not much, only enough for the paper and the printing costs. He paid the authors so little that the very thought of it makes me laugh at myself. And when the Devil's money ran out the unfortunate fellow went to Tashkent and found a new publisher. This one wasn't a devil or an unfortunate. He was a crook.

I've seen some scoundrels in the course of my terrible life, I can tell you, sweet friend. I've been fleeced. But I've never met a rascal like that. If anyone like that were to cross my path now, I would no doubt emerge unscathed, for I have grown sadder and wiser — I know people and beware of them now, but in those days... Good God! It was not a face, my dear fellow, it was a passport. And anyway who, I ask you, who but a wishy-washy intellectual would dream of signing a contract with a man whose surname was Grabkin! No, I didn't make it up! Grabkin! A puny fellow in pinstriped trousers and a cherry-coloured tie with an imitation pearl pin, grimy fingernails, and eyes...

But the editor, ah, the editor!

I went to see him.

"Now then, old boy," he said, "go along to Grabkin's office and sign a contract with him. Everything's been sorted out. It's just fine."

"Now listen, Rudolph Raphailovich," I replied. "I've seen Grabkin. I'm afraid of him. He's got an imitation pin in his tie, Rudolph Raphailovich. I'd rather sign a contract with you."

He smiled. He's a strong man, a real Toreador from Granada.

He drew a circle on a piece of paper and said:

"My child! You're so inexperienced, like all writers. See this circle? It's you."

A second circle appeared on the piece of paper.

"This is me, the editor."

"Hmm."

The third circle turned out to be Grabkin the publisher.

"Now look. I'm going to join the writer with the editor and the publisher. See?"

This produced a geometrical figure, an isosceles triangle.

"There's a thread from the publisher to me and another one from him to the writer. You and I have only literary connections: we know how to read a manuscript or talk about Gogol, but we can't and won't enter into any financial calculations. I can talk to you about Anatole France, but not to Grabkin... no, not to him, because he doesn't know who Anatole France is. But I can't talk to you about money, for two reasons — firstly, a writer is not supposed to be interested in money, and, secondly, you don't understand the first thing about it. Contracts are signed with publishers, old boy, not with editors, and, what's more Grabkin is off to the People's Commissariat for Education at two thirty precise, and it's a quarter to two now, so get a move on, and don't sit around here looking wobbly and scared stiff..."

It was on the tip of my tongue to say "Then why did I sign my first contract with you?" But as I put on my threadbare old coat in the hall, I asked in a hollow voice:

"But have you seen his eyes? He's got triangular eyelids and steely eyes that look sideways."

To which he replied:

"The next publisher I get will have eyes like yours, crystal clear. You've been spoilt, you know. Read what you are going to sign carefully, and the promissory note as well."

I shall not describe the office of Semyon Semyonovich Grabkin to you, my friend. I shall merely say that I was surprised to see the sign "Photographic goods". What had this to do with novels? Even more astounding was the fact that there were no photographic goods whatsoever in the office. There were five small packages, the top one of which had been opened, and on these I read the word "Phenacetin". Phenacetin, as you know, my friend, is, of course, para-acet-phenitidin, and can be used in photography in one case only, namely, if the photographer has a headache. Actually I know nothing at all about photography, and the main point of interest was not this, but the hundred or so tins of sprats lying in the other corner. So, according to the editor, Grabkin was going to the Commissariat for Education at two thirty. Was it to offer them the sprats? Or had the Commissariat given him the sprats, while he was going to complain that they were going off?

Grabkin's office was crammed with people. All wearing hats and upset about something. I kept hearing the words "promissory note", "Shapiro" and "red tape".

Grabkin received me as if I were a ghost. I had the impression that he was scared of me. I can say for sure that he was desperate not to sign either the promissory note or the contract — from what he said it seemed that both the contract and the promissory note were a mere formality and surely I didn't think he wouldn't pay me? Just imagine, for a moment I actually hesitated... I can see you stamp your foot. He wanted me to give him permission in writing to print my novel. You're laughing? Wait a minute. I managed to be firm. I felt myself turn pale and walked over to the door. He brought me back, shrugging his shoulders painfully, and under the disapproving glances of all and sundry sent someone off to the shop for some promissory note-paper. To cut a long story short, I emerged from the office an hour later with a contract in my pocket together with four promissory notes for four miserly sums. I was terribly ashamed of myself for having taken a promissory note from Grabkin. Here was I, a writer, with promissory notes in my pocket!

You are an impatient, hot-blooded person and will, of course, know what happened next, namely, Grabkin disappeared a month later, the promissory notes turned out to be forged, he wasn't Grabkin at all, the novel never got published...

No, no, it wasn't like that. Nothing so primitive. It was much worse. I shall not tell a lie. I received money on all four promissory notes, not the whole amount, true, but somewhat less (they were bought from me before they expired), and my novel was published, but not in full, only the first half! Grabkin did disappear, but on the same day, not a month later. And he did not go off to the Commissariat for Education, as I learnt later, but to catch a train. And I haven't seen him since, you know, (although I hope I shall sooner or later, if I remain alive).

But all because I turned up at Grabkin's office on that dusty day and, like a lunatic, put my signature next to his, I:

1) was visited three times at my flat by goodness-knows-who,

2) went to the bank three times,

3) went to see a solicitor,

4) went somewhere else too, and

5) took the editor to an arbitration court. What is more, the five middle-aged men who examined the agreements, mine with the editor, the editor's with the unfortunate fellow, mine with Grabkin and the editor's with Grabkin, ended up in a frenzy. Solomon himself could not have said who owned the novel, and why the novel was only half-published, who the sprats in the office belonged to and where Grabkin was.

Yet one thing they did manage to work out: that by signing this enslaving agreement I had surrendered my novel to a certain Grabkin, that the whereabouts of Grabkin were unknown, but that Grabkin had proxies in Moscow and, consequently, my novel was buried for the next three years and I did not have the right to sell it a second time. In the end I burst out laughing and wrote it off.

A curious detail: I saw the name S.S. Grabkin in the telephone directory with my own eyes. Yet when the court hearing took place and I looked in the same telephone directory I couldn't find Grabkin anywhere.

I swear to God — I'm telling the truth!

This really gave me a turn. How can you remove your name from all the Moscow telephone directories?

Now I shall run ahead somewhat: a few years later, as you will have guessed, Grabkin was found abroad. In possession of my novel and play. How he managed to take the novel with him, I don't know, since it was heavy as a tombstone.

Actually I'm ashamed of myself. Such sloppiness is quite unforgivable. But listen to the rest of it. One fine day, like a bombshell, I heard the news that my editor had been arrested and forced to leave the country. And he did in fact disappear. But now I'm sure he wasn't deported, the man simply sank into oblivion, like a penny in a pond. All sorts of people were deported or simply vanished to various spots around the globe in those famous years from 1921 to 1925! Yet, say someone went to Mexico. What could be further away, you might think. Then you'd suddenly be sent a photo of a pancake Russian face under a cactus. And it was him! But they say this fellow was only sent to Berlin, not to Mexico. And there wasn't a word from him. Not a peep. He wasn't in Berlin at all. He just couldn't be.

It was some time before the matter was cleared up. One day I met a very clever man. And told him the whole story. After which he smiled and said:

"You know what, that Rudolph of yours was carried off by the Devil, and so was Grabkin."

I suddenly saw the light. Of course, that's what had happened.

"And it was quite simple. You said yourself that Rudolph had sold his soul to the Devil."

"Yes, that's right."

"Well, his time was up, so the Devil came along and said, "Off we go, old chap..."

"Oh, heavens! Where are they now then?"

Instead of replying he pointed to the ground. It gave me the creeps.

III. A FIT OF WEAKNESS FAUST IS QUITE IMMORTAL. LIKE THE SAARDAM CARPENTER NEURASTHENIA

I had a frightening dream. There was a bitter frost, and the iron cross on the St Vladimir was burning incredibly high up over the frozen Dnieper.

And I saw a man, a Jew. He was kneeling down, and a pockmarked officer was hitting him on the head with a cleaning rod, and black blood was trickling down the Jew's face. He bent under the steel rod, and in my dream I understood clearly that his name was Furman, that he was a tailor and that he was innocent, and I began to cry and shout in my sleep!

"Don't you dare, scoundrel!"

And the soldiers fell on me at once, and the pock-marked man shouted:

"Do 'im in!"

I was dying in my dream. In an instant I decided it was better to shoot myself than be tortured to death and I rushed over to a pile of firewood. But as always in dreams the Browning would not fire and I cried out, gasping.

I woke up sobbing and shivered for a long time in the dark until I realised that I was in Moscow, an awfully long way from Vladimir, in my squalid room, that it was the night muttering around me, that it was 1923 and the pock-marked man had long since left the land of the living.

Limping, hardly stepping with my painful foot, I dragged myself over to the lamp and lit it. It revealed the poverty and meanness of my life. I saw my cat's alarmed yellow pupils. I had found her a year ago by the gate. She was pregnant. A man passing by, perfectly sober, kicked her in the belly, and the woman at the gate saw him do it. The dumb bleeding animal gave birth to two dead kittens and was ill for a long time in my room, but did not die. I nursed her. The cat lived with me, but was afraid and took a long time to get used to me. My room was right under the roof and arranged in such a way that I could let her out to walk on the roof in summer and winter. I didn't let her into the corridor of the communal flat, for I was afraid I might be sent to prison because of her. One day some ruffians stopped me in a dark alley by Patriarch Ponds. I instinctively clutched at my pocket, then remembered it had been empty for several years. So I bought a hunting knife at Sukharev market from a suspicious-looking character and have carried it on me ever since. I was afraid that if anyone hit the cat again, I would end up in prison.

Seeing that I had got up, she grew miserable, opened her eyes and watched me moodily and suspiciously. I stared at the worn oil-cloth, reopening old wounds. I remembered being insulted by someone twelve years ago when I was still very young. The insult had remained unavenged. Suddenly I wanted to go to the town where he lived and challenge him to a duel. Then I remembered that he had been rotting in the grave for many years and his remains were not even to be found. Memories of two more insults crept painfully into my mind. They brought with them others that I myself had inflicted on creatures weaker than I. Then all the scars in my heart seemed to catch fire. I looked longingly at the light flex. It was hanging down invitingly. I lay my head on the oil-cloth and thought how hopeless my position was. Life had suddenly drifted away like smoke, and here I was in Moscow, completely alone in a room, and what's more, with this ill-treated smoky cat to look after, what's more. Each day I had to buy it ten-kopecks' worth of meat and let it in and out. And on top of that it gave birth three times a year, each time most painfully, and I had to help it, then pay to have one of the kittens drowned, and train the other one, then beg someone in the house to take it and not ill-treat it.

A burden, a burden.

And what was the reason for it all?

The crazy idea of dropping everything and taking up writing instead.

I groaned and went over to the divan. The light disappeared. The springs sang congestedly in the dark. The insults and misfortunes gradually melted away.

Then came another dream. But the frost was not so bitter, and big, soft snowflakes were falling. Everything was white. And I realised that it was Christmas. A bay trotter covered with a mauve rug came round the corner.

"Whoa!" shouted the driver in my dream. I threw off the travelling rug, gave the driver some money, opened the soundless solid door to the entrance-hall and began climbing up the staircase.

It was warm in the large apartment. Goodness me, what a lot of rooms! More than you could count, and solid seductive things in each of them. My younger brother detached himself from the piano. He beckoned to me, laughing. In spite of the fact that his chest had a bullet hole covered with black plaster, I started gabbling away, breathless with happiness.

"So your wound's healed, has it?" I asked.

"Oh, perfectly."

The score of Faust stood on the piano above the open keyboard, it was open at the page of*Valentin's aria.*

"And the lung's not affected?"

"O, what lung?"

"Then sing the cavatina."

He began singing.

Warmth billowed from the central heating, the electric light bulbs shone in the chandelier, and out came Sofie in patent leather shoes. I hugged her.

Then I sat on my divan and wiped my tear-stained face. I wanted to see a sorcerer who could interpret dreams. But I could understand this dream even without a sorcerer.

The mauve rug on the trotter was taken from 1913, a brilliant, sumptuous year. But the bullet-torn breast was wrong, that came much later, 1919. And my brother could not have been in that flat. I was the one who lived there once. At Christmas I went arm in arm with Sofie to the cinema. The snow crunched under her shoes, and Sofie laughed.

In any case, the black plaster, the dream laugh and Valentin could mean only one thing — my brother, whom I had last seen at the very beginning of 1919, had been killed. When and where I do not know and probably never shall. He had been killed, so all that remained of everything that shone, Sofie, the lights, Zhenya and the mauve pompons, was me on a tattered divan in Moscow that night in 1923. The rest had perished.

The night was quiet. There was a smell of mould. One thing I could not understand was why I had dreamed of warmth. It was cold in my room.

"I'm going to pieces," I thought, shuddering. My heart kept plunging down and resurfacing. "I must find some bromide."

I put on my shabby slippers with a sigh. Something pricked my heel. A drawing pin had fallen into my slipper. "Let it prick me, that would ease my heart."

My old silk night-shirt had served me too long. It had split into vertical strips, but I treasured it as a memento. I pulled on my coat over my nightshirt and began crawling, literally crawling over to the table.

"I wonder at exactly what point I shall die. Before I get to the table or after? When I get to the table I must write a note — but what shall I say? Rubbish! Shouldn't I give in? It's just nicotine poisoning and now this longing, this fear of death."

At any event I did not die on the way to the table. I began to die at the table. The cat had been watching me for some time.

"Will anyone take you in, creature?"

"Murochka! Please look after my cat and don't let Buldin ill-treat it..."

My hands were cold and covered with cold sweat. I wouldn't have time to finish the note.

But I did have time to write:

"In return for this I leave all the things in my room to my neighbour Maria Potapovna Klyonova."

It would have been easier just to shout "Murochka". But I was ashamed and embarrassed. I would wake not only Murochka but also Tarakanov and his wife. Ugh, how disgusting!

I restrained myself.

"It's death from a heart attack," I thought and felt that death was insulting me. Death in this room — ugh... They would come in... making a din... no money to pay for the funeral. In Moscow, on the fifth floor, all alone... Not a respectable death.

Much better to die in an apartment on clean sweet-smelling sheets or on a battle-field. Just dig your head into the ground, then they'd crawl over to you, lift you up and turn you over to face the sun, but your eyes would be glassy already.

But death still didn't come.

"Bromide? What for? Bromide can't prevent a heart attack, can it?"

All the same I put one hand down to the bottom drawer, opened it and began rummaging around, holding my heart with my left hand. I did not find the bromide, but discovered two phenacetin powders and several old photographs. Instead of bromide, I drank some water from the cold kettle, after which I felt that death had been postponed for a bit.

An hour passed. The house was still silent, and I felt as if I were alone in the whole of Moscow in my stone sack. My heart had calmed down, and my expectation of death already seemed shameful. I moved the barrack-like lamp as close as possible to the table and put a pink paper cover over its green shade, which brightened it up. On it I wrote the words "And the dead were judged out of those things which were written in the books, according to their works." Then I began to write, not knowing what would come of it. I remember wanting very much to convey how good it is to be in a warm house with a clock in the dining room that strikes the hour, to be lying drowsily in bed, to write about books, and frost, and the terrible pock-marked man, and my dreams. Writing's pretty difficult in general, but for some reason this seemed easy. I had no intention of publishing it at all.

I got up from the table when I heard the hoarse coughing of old Semyonovna in the corridor, a woman I whole-heartedly detested for the way she maltreated her son, twelve-year-old Shurik. Even now, six years later, I still hate her.

I pulled the curtain and saw that I no longer needed the lamp on. It was growing light outside. The clock said a quarter past seven. I had sat at the table for five hours.

IV. THREE LIVES

After that each night at one o'clock I sat down at the table and wrote until three or four in the morning. It was easy at night. In the morning I had to explain myself to my old neighbour Semyonovna.

"Yer at it again. 'Ad the light on last night, didn't yer?"

"Yes, I did."

"Yer know the electricity's not supposed to be turned on at night."

"That's precisely when it is meant to be on."

"There's only one metre for the lot of us. We all have to pay."

"I don't use the light between five and midnight."

"And why do folk stay up all night, I'd like to know. We don't have no tsar now."

"I'm printing ten-rouble banknotes."

"What?"

"Printing counterfeit banknotes, ten-rouble ones."

"Don't yer make fun of me. We've got a house committee to take care of gents with smart hair-dos. They can be packed off to where the hintellectuals belong. We workers ain't got no use for all that writing."

"A woman who sells homemade toffee at Smolensk market is more of a private tradesman than a worker."

"Yer leave my toffee alone. We've never lived in a mansion. It's about time you was evicted."

"Talking about eviction, Semyonovna. If you start clouting Shurik round the head once more and I hear that tormented child shouting, I'll complain about you to the people's court, and you'll get three months in prison, but if I had my way it would be more."

In order to write at night, you must have some means of subsistence in the daytime. How I existed from 1921 to 1923 I shall not begin to tell you. For one thing, you wouldn't believe me and, for another, it's irrelevant to the matter in hand.

But by 1923 I managed to find a way of subsisting.

In one of my quite fantastic jobs I became friendly with a very likeable journalist by the name of Abram.

Abram grabbed me by the sleeve in the street and took me to the editorial office of the big newspaper where he worked. On his instructions I offered my services as a processor. That was their name for people who turned illiterate material into literate copy suitable for printing.

I was given some correspondence from the provinces and rewrote it. It was taken away somewhere, then Abram appeared with a sad expression in his eyes and, not knowing where to look, told me that I had been found unsuitable.

I cannot for the life of me remember why a few days later I submitted myself to a second ordeal. My memory is a complete blank. But I do recall that about a week later I was sitting at a grimy wobbly-legged table in the editorial office, writing and mentally cursing Abram.

I can tell you one thing, my friend, that I have never had a more revolting job in my whole life. Even now I still have bad dreams about it. A stream of excruciating grey boredom, constant and relentless. Outside it was raining.

Again I cannot recall why I was asked to write sketches. It had nothing to do with my re-writing. On the contrary, I kept expecting to get the sack because, strictly entre nous, I was a very bad worker, careless and lazy, and detested my work.

It is possible (and indeed seems likely) that what helped me was that illustrious and inimitable newspaper, Sochelnik. It came out in Berlin, and I wrote humorous sketches for it. The newspaper had a representative in Moscow, a lady who was all silk and rings.................

"This item would be better turned into a humorous sketch."

The managing editor stared at me in surprise.

"But you can't do that, can you?"

I coughed.

"Have a try," the managing editor suddenly said decisively.

I had a try. I really couldn't tell you what it was all about. Some step-ladder in a library was covered with ice and the assistants kept falling down with the books. It was published the next day. And that was just the beginning.

One fine day who should drop in but the deputy editor-in-chief, a nice chap though a bit of a fanatic, who went by the nickname July.

"It isn't you who writes those sketches for *Sochelnik*, is it, Mikhail?" he asked.

I went pale and decided that my end had come. *Sochelnik* enjoyed the unanimous contempt of all and sundry: it was despised by emigre monarchists, Moscow non-party members and, most important, by the Communists. In short, it was the world's worst newspaper.

I blanched. But it turned out that July wanted me to write the same good sketches as I did for *Sochelnik*. I explained that unfortunately this was impossible, that the style of *Sochelnik* was quite different and so were the sketches in it, but that I would do my best to ensure that the sketches in July's paper were good too.

Then came a contract. I was put on a salary higher than a processor's, in return for which I undertook to write eight short sketches a month. So that was that.

And I began writing...

All this was fine, but there was one snag. Now I will tell you another secret: to write a sketch of seventy-five to a hundred lines long took me from eighteen to twenty-two minutes, smoking and whistling included. To get it typed out, eight minutes, giggling with a typist included. In short, half-an-hour for the whole thing. I signed the sketch either with some stupid pen name or occasionally for some reason with my real name and took it either to July or to another deputy with the unusual surname of Navzikat.

This Navzikat went on plaguing me for about three years. It took me three days to get the hang of him. He was incompetent, for one thing. Rude, for another. And arrogant, for a third. With the non-party employees under him he behaved aggressively, insulting them by his constant suspicious. He had no idea how to run a newspaper. So why he had been appointed to such a responsible post I really cannot say.

Navzikat would begin by twiddling the sketch around and looking for some criminal idea in it concerning the Soviet regime. Having convinced himself that there was no obvious harm in it, he proceeded to give advice and correct the sketch.

During all this my nerves were on edge and I smoked furiously, feeling a strong urge to hit him on the head with the ashtray.

After spoiling the sketch to the best of his ability, Navzikat wrote "Type-set" on it, and my working day came to an end. After that I concentrated my mind on one idea only, how to beat a hasty retreat. Unfortunately July cherished the forlorn hope that all the staff, including the sketch writers, would arrive on the dot every morning and sit to the bitter end in the editorial office, striving to render unto the state all they could. At the slightest deviation from this the honest July began to lose weight and pine away.

Whereas I cherished the fond hope of slipping out of the office and going home to my room, which I hated like poison, but which had a precious pile of paper in it. There was actually no point at all in my staying in the office. So I tried to kill time. Stiff with boredom, I drifted from room to room, chatting with the staff, listening to jokes and smoking myself silly.

Finally, having killed an hour or two, I took to my heels.

And so, my friend, I lived a triple life. One at the newspaper. Daylight. Pouring with rain. Boredom. Navzikat. July. My head aching and empty as I left.

Life two. In the afternoon after the newspaper I trudged over to the Moscow branch of the *Sochelnik* editorial office. This second life was more to my taste than the first. I could at least develop a few of my ideas there.

I must tell you that during this second life I wrote about a hundred printed pages. A short novel? No, not a novel, more like a collection of memoirs.

I actually got an extract from this work of art published in the literary supplement to *Sochelnik*. Another extract I sold most successfully to the owner of a grocer's shop. He was passionately fond of literature and in order to publish a novel he had written entitled *The Villian*, he brought out a whole almanach. This included the grocer's novel, a story by Jack London, some other stories by Soviet writers and the extract by yours truly. And he actually paid his authors. Partly in money and partly in sprats. It was then, I should point out, that I first came up against the censor. Everything was fine for the others, but in my case the censor deleted several lines. When these lines were removed, the work acquired an enigmatic, meaningless and, undoubtedly, more counter-revolutionary nature. Things went from bad to worse. No matter how much I ran around Moscow trying to sell someone a chunk of my work, I achieved nothing. No one was tempted either by the chunk or by the whole work. One editor even said he thought what I had written was counter-revolutionary and strongly advised me not to write anything else like it. I was filled with dark forebodings, but they soon passed. *Sochelnik* came to the rescue. After reading what I had written, one of the bosses of that organ, a man with a yellow briefcase made from the skin of some tropical reptile, expressed the desire to print my work in full.

Taking advantage of my impecunity and the autumn slush, the *Sochelnik* branch offered me eight dollars (sixteen roubles) per twenty-five pages. I remember my mixed feelings of shame and helpless fury as I received a slim pile of multicoloured Soviet banknotes whose value then was steadily falling. I waited three months for the manuscript to come out before realising that it would not. Then I found out the reason — my story had received a black mark from the censor. They spent ages chewing it over with various people in Moscow and Berlin.

Meanwhile the frosts came. The whole of Moscow was frozen. One evening I went round to the *Sochelnik* office in my light cloth coat and whom should I see there but Rudolph. He was sitting there with wet eyelashes in a nice fur coat. We started talking.

"Aren't you writing anything?" Rudolph asked.

I told him about my story. It was common knowledge that Rudolph only liked publishing people who had already made a name for themselves. He ran his magazine (then still a slim one) very cleverly.

"Let's have a look at it," Rudolph said to me, with a condescending smile.

I took the manuscript out of my pocket at once (I even slept with it). Rudolph read all one hundred pages sitting there in his fur coat and said:

"You know what? I'll publish an extract."

I did my best not to betray my delight to Rudolph, but couldn't help it, of course. For me, a man wearing a light cloth coat in winter, it was most gratifying to have something published by Rudolph.

Honesty always leads to something unpleasant. I have always known that crooks, for one thing, live better than honest folk and, for another, enjoy universal respect. All the same I couldn't restrain myself from warning Rudolph that no one wanted to publish the piece because they were afraid of the censor. Then I got scared that Rudolph would hand the manuscript back to me. But to my surprise this information made not the slightest impression on him. I remember that he paid me something for the extract and I soon saw it in print. This gave me enormous satisfaction, as did the fact that my name was included in the list of contributors on the cover of the magazine.

I am relating this unremarkable incident to you, so that you know how I became acquainted with Rudolph.

Then winter really got going. A triple life. My third life flourished at the writing desk. The pile of paper grew plumper. I wrote now in pencil and now in ink.

Meanwhile the sketches for the newspaper were taking their toll. By the end of winter this became quite clear. My taste had declined drastically. Trite words and hackneyed comparisons crept into my screeds with increasing frequency. Each sketch had to contain a stray element of ridicule, and this led to coarseness. Whenever I tried to make the sketch a little subtler, a perplexed air appeared on the face of Navzikat, my executioner. In the end I gave up and tried to write in a way that Navzikat would think was funny. The sketches that I composed there would make your hair stand on end, my friend.

Whenever some revolutionary anniversary was approaching, Navzikat used to say:

"I hope you'll come up with a nice heroic story for the celebrations the day after tomorrow."

I turned white, then red, and hummed and hawed.

'"I don't know how to write heroic revolutionary stories," I told Navzikat.

Navzikat couldn't understand that. As I had long since realised, he had a strange idea about journalists and writers. He assumed that a journalist could write anything you wanted them to, and wouldn't care what he wrote. For various reasons there were certain things that I could not explain to Navzikat: for example, that in order to come up with a nice revolutionary story you had, first of all, to be a revolutionary and be looking forward to the revolutionary celebrations in question. If someone came up with a story for financial or some other trivial motives, it was bound to be bad. As you will appreciate, I did not mention this to Navzikat. July was cleverer and more subtle and realised without being told that I was incapable of producing heroic stories. His shaven head became clouded with sorrow. What is more, as a means of self-defence, I stole a sketch at the end of the third month and another two at the end of the fourth, handing in seven and six respectively.

"Mikhail," July said, devastated, "you've only done six sketches."

"Is it really only six?" I asked in surprise. "So it is. You know, July, I've been having a lot of migraines recently."

"It's all that beer," July interjected quickly.

"It's not the beer, it's the sketches."

"For goodness' sake, Mikhail. You spend two hours a week writing a sketch."

"But if only you knew what those two hours take out of me, my dear fellow!"

"I don't get it... What's the matter with you!"

Navzikat tried to come to July's aid. Ideas were welling up in his head like bubbles.

"I hope you'll be able to do a sketch on the French minister."

I began to feel dizzy.

I'll explain to you, my friend, and you will understand: how can you write a good sketch about a French minister if you don't give a damn about him? Note the automatic assumption — you are supposed to show the minister in a ridiculous and unfavourable light and tear him to pieces. But a writer can only produce a good political sketch if he really detests the minister. That's elementary, isn't it? Yes?

Alright then, let's compose one.

"The minister went into his office and phoned..."

And — stop. What next?

Well, phoned his secretary. And what did he say to him?

To cut a long story short, in the end they left me alone. Navzikat in the firm conviction that I was a small-scale counter-revolutionary agent engaged in a spot of minor sabotage, July on the grounds that I was a deeply unhappy bohemian, idler and lost sheep. Neither of them was right, but one was nearer the truth.

Overjoyed at having rid myself of French ministers and Ruhr miners forever, I stole three sketches that month, handing in five. I am ashamed to confess that the next month I produced only four. At this point July lost his patience and put me on piece work. I must confess that this upset me greatly. I wanted the state to pay me a salary so that I could do nothing but lie on the floor in my room writing a novel. But the state can't do that, as I realise only too well....................................

V. IT'S FINISHED

At that moment something strange happened. Someone started playing the overture to "Faust" in the flat downstairs. I was flabbergasted. There was a piano downstairs, but no one had played it for a long time. The sombre chords floated up to me. I lay on the floor, my face almost touching the glass of the oil-stove, and looked at hell. My despair was total. I thought about my awful life and knew that now at last it was about to cease.

Images flashed into my head: the Devil had come to the despairing Faust, but no one would come to me. A shameful fear of death shot through me once more, but I tried to overcome it by imagining what awaited me if I did not have the courage to do it. First of all, I pictured the dirty corridor of our communal flat, the disgusting common lavatory and the screams of the tormented Shurka. This helped a lot and, gritting my teeth, I put the barrel to my temple. The touch of the cold metal on my skin produced another wave of fear. "No one will come to the rescue," I thought bitterly. The deep and mysterious sounds drifted up through the floor. There was a knock at the door just as my cowardly finger was cautiously groping for the trigger. Thanks to this knock I almost did put a bullet through my head, because the unexpectedness of it made my hand shake and press the trigger.

But God, omnipresent, saved me from sin. My automatic pistol had no safety catch. In order to fire it you had not only to press the trigger, but clutch the whole revolver hard in your hand so that the second release pressed down on the butt from the back. One without the other would not produce a shot. And I had forgotten about the second.

There was another knock.

Thrusting the revolver hastily into my pocket, I crumpled up my note, hid it and called out sternly:

"Come in! Who's there?"

VI. DRESSED IN MY SWORD!

The door opened soundlesly and the Devil appeared on the threshold. The son of perdition was transformed, however. All that remained of his customary attire was a black velvet beret pulled jauntily over one ear. There was no cock's feather. And instead of a cloak, he was wearing a fox-lined coat and ordinary tight-fitting striped trousers on his legs, of which one had a hoof concealed in a shiny galosh.

Quaking with fear, I stared at my guest. My teeth were chattering.

A patch of crimson light lit the face of the visitor from below, and I realised that the evil one had decided to appear to me in the form of his servant Rudolph.

"Hello," said Satan in surprise, taking off his beret and galoshes.

"Hello," I replied, still rooted to the spot.

"Why are you lying on the floor?" the Devil enquired.

"Oh, it's the oil store... you see..." I mumbled.

"Hm!" said Beelzebub.

"Do sit down, please."

"Merci. Couldn't you light the lamp?"

"The bulb's gone, you see, and it's too late now to..."

The Devil smiled, opened his briefcase and took out an electric light bulb in a grey cylindrical packet.

"Do you always carry light bulbs around with you?"

The Devil gave a condescending smile.

"Pure coincidence," he replied, "just bought it."

I screwed in the bulb, and an unpleasant light lit up the room.

My quaking stopped, and I said suddenly:

"You know, just before you came... hm... can you hear, they're playing Faust..."

"Yes, I can hear it!"

There was a pause.

"I was just passing," the Devil said, "and I thought to myself, why don't I drop in."

"Very kind of you. Would you care for some tea?"

The Devil refused the tea.

There was a pause.

"Finished your novel?" the Devil asked suddenly.

I started up.

"How did you know?"

"Busin told me."

"Hm... I haven't read it to Busin. Who is this Busin anyway?"

"Someone I happen to know," the Devil replied, with a yawn.

"Yes, I have finished it," I said, suffering.

"Let's have a look at it," said Satan in a bored voice. "I've got a moment or two."

"You know it hasn't been typed yet and my writing's terrible. I write the letter 'a' like an 'o', understand, so it's..."

"That's quite common," said Mephistopheles, with a yawn. "I can read any hand-writing. I'm used to it. Which drawer is it in? This one?"

"I've changed my mind about trying to get it published, you see."

"Why?" asked Rudolph, screwing up his eyes.

"The censor won't allow it."

"How do you know?"

"I've been told."

"Who told you?"

"Boozkin. Moankin, Parsov..."

"Parsov, that little chap?"

"Yes, with the blond hair."

"I'm not talking about publication," the Evil One explained, "it's just out of curiosity. I like good literature."

"Actually... I don't think much of this..." And without realising it I found myself opening the drawer.

The Devil took off his fur coat, hung it on a nail, put on his pince-nez, transforming himself finally into Rudolph and picked up the first notebook. His eyes started racing along the lines. It was true. From the way he was turning over the pages I realised that the worst handwriting in the world could not stop him. He was reading it as if it were in print.

Four hours passed. During those four hours the Evil One took refreshment once only. He ate a piece of roll with sausage and drank a glass of tea. When the hands on the clock stood on guard, dead on midnight, Rudolph read the final words about the stars and closed the fifth and last notebook. My torment was at an end. While it was going on I had re-read volume one of "The Pickwick Papers". I tried not to look Rudolph in the eye, not to give myself away by a cowardly or pathetic glance. But my eyes would not stay still.

"He didn't like it. The corners of his mouth have turned down in disgust," I thought, "poor me... Why on earth did I let him read it?"

"It's just a draft, you know, I haven't edited it yet."

Ugh, just listen to my loathsome voice...

"Has your mother died?" Rudolph asked.

"Yes," I replied in amazement.

"When?"

"My mother died the year before last from typhus, to my great grief," I said bleakly.

The Devil registerd an expression of polite official condolence on his face.

"And would you mind telling me where you were educated?"

"At a parish school." I said the first thing that came into my head. The fact was, you see, that at that time I thought it necessary for some reason to keep quiet about my higher education. I was ashamed that a person with such an education should work on a newspaper, lie on the floor in front of an oil-stove and not have any pictures hanging on the wall.

"I see," Rudolph said, and his eyes gleamed.

"Forgive me, but what is the point of these questions?"

"You're imitating Count Tolstoy," the Devil announced, tapping the notebook with his finger.

"Precisely which Tolstoy," I enquired, irritated by Rudolph's enigmatic questions. "Lev Nikolayevich, Alexei Konstantinovich or perhaps the even more famous Pyotr Andreyevich who lured Prince Alexei into a trap?"

"Well, I never!" exclaimed Rudolph. "Don't be angry. But tell me, are you a monarchist?"

I turned white as death, as befits anyone asked such a question.

"God forbid!" I cried.

The Devil screwed up his eyes cunningly and asked:

"Tell me, how many times a week do you shave?"

"Seven," I replied, at a loss.

"So you sit by an oil-stove," the Devil looked round the room. "Alone with a cat and an oil-stove, shave once a day... And forgive me if I ask another question: how do you manage to get a parting like that?"

"I put brioline on my hair," I replied sullenly, "but not everyone who puts brioline on his hair is necessarily a monarchist."

"Oh, I'm not interfering with your convictions," the Devil retorted. Then he paused, raised his eyes to the smoke-blackened ceiling and murmured: "Puts brioline on..."

Then his intonation changed. His pince-nez flashing sternly, he said in a funereal voice:

"No one will publish your novel. Rimsky won't, nor will Agreyev. And I advise you not to even offer it to them."

The smoky beast came out of a corner and rubbed itself against my leg.

"What a life we have, you and I, cat, what a life," I thought sadly and wilted.

"There's only one person in the world who can publish it," Rudolph continued, "and that person is me!"

A chill passed under my heart, and I listened, but there was no sound of Faust now. The house was asleep.

"I'll print it in my magazine and even in book form later. I'll pay you well, too".

Then he named a monstrously small sum.

"I'll even give you fifty roubles in advance now."

I said nothing.

"With the following request," he began again. "Couldn't you soak your parting out for a week? I'd even advise you as a friend not to wear it at all. And would you mind not shaving this week?"

I gaped in amazement.

"It will be typed out tomorrow," Rudolph said, pensively.

"But there are over four hundred pages!" I exclaimed fearfully. "How can it be typed tomorrow?"

"Tomorrow at nine a.m.," replied the Devil in an iron voice, "I shall take it to the typing pool and get twelve typists, divide it into twelve bits and they will have it typed by the evening."

I realised that it was not for me to argue with him. I lay admiringly at his feet.

"That'll cost about a hundred and fifty roubles, to be paid by the author, note. The day after tomorrow I'll take it to the censor in the morning, and three days after that you and I will go there together."

"I see," I said in a deathly voice.

"You won't say a single word there, and no partings either," said Rudolph sternly.

At this I made a feeble attempt to rebel.

"Am I really such an idiot that I can't be trusted to open my mouth? And if I am, you go there alone. Why do you need me?"

"I'll tell you why," Rudolph continued in an icy voice. "He'll decide to strike something out. Precisely what, I don't know. Although I've got a good idea. So you'll give your full consent to whatever he says. And it would even be a good thing if you paid him some kind of compliment. Like how clever of him to suggest it and you, the author, think your novel is ten times better with all those bits cut out."

"I hate the sound of it," I muttered and launched into a tirade against censorship. It lasted about five minutes. Rudolph sprawled on the tatty divan, his little eyes squinting with pleasure. I closed my mouth at last.

"Have you finished?"

"Yes, I have."

"My child!" Rudolph said, taking a red six-faceted pencil out and deleting "From the Apocalypse" in the epigraph.

"You needn't have done that," I said, looking over his shoulder. "He'll probably know where it's from anyway, won't he?"

"He doesn't know a blasted thing," Rudolph replied morosely, then skimmed through all five notebooks and crossed out another six or so phrases, each time enquiring politely "May I?"

Then he handed me five ten-rouble notes, after which his beret and my novel disappeared through the floor. I thought I saw a wisp of a flame leap out from a block of parquet, and the room smelt of sulphur for a long while. Or maybe I just imagined it.

A long time after the light bulb left as a present to me had gone out and the cat fallen asleep on the newspapers, I stood by the window looking out into the dark. My house was sailing like a multi-decked ship with its black sails flying. A misty mish-mash was stewing overhead.

I fell asleep eventually and dreamed of cadets in 1918. Hundreds of them were marching alone, whistling and singing a wild song. I don't know about the cat's dreams. It probably dreamt about dogs, but perhaps people too. And that's far more frightening.

VII. A WASHED-OUT PHOTOGRAPH

What happened afterwards you know, precious friend, from what was written earlier: the man with the corn, sprats and promissory notes who went bust, Grabkin and all that nonsense. About everything else my mind is a total blank. Can't remember a thing! It rained, I think. And there was the boredom too, I was tormented by a stupifying boredom. It spread everywhere, creeping into me and making my blood rot. I remember the fag ends and spit on Strastnaya Square, some women with wet hems, Navzikat. My leg hurting as I limped to the newspaper. Walk past it! Past it!

VIII. THE NOVEL IS PUBLISHED

Nevertheless the day came on which I faltered. When the lamps and street-lights went on and the block pavements glistened, I went to Grabkin's office. And this will show you how blank my mind has gone, because I can't remember whether it was spring, or summer perhaps. Or February? February? Can't remember.

Everything in his office had changed. There were no sprats and no Grabkin, but some hard board partitions had gone up, and Rudolph presided in one of these boxes under a dazzling light. In front of him in two piles lay new copies of the magazine just printed. Their blue covers looked very elegant. Rudolph was beaming and greeted me with a warm handshake.

In front of Rudolph sat a young man of a very particular type. I have met them frequently at editorial offices. Their identification marks are as follows. Age — twenty-five to thirty. Never more nor less. Well-dressed. A jacket, and sometimes a morning coat too, but an old one. Trousers always pinstriped. Always wearing a tie, either a long cherry-coloured one or a check bow tie. Always with a cane, a silver-topped one. And always with a smart hair-cut. Who they are nobody knows. Who are their parents? What do they do for a living? They write nothing themselves. When asked what their surname is, the editor replies, with a frown:

"Surname? Pi... dammit, I've forgotten!"

They are always to be found in editorial offices on special days, the day when a new issue comes out, days of great literary scandals, days when magazines are closed down. In particular they like whispering with women in editorial offices, are very polite to them and refer to all People's Commissars by their first name and patronymic.

So they don't say:

"People's commissar so-and-so."

Or

"C(omrade) so-and-so."

But:

"Anatoly Vassilievich told us yesterday and we had a good laugh..."

From which one gathers that they hobnob with People's Commissars, does one? I don't know.

In short, he was already sitting there.

I sat down too.

Rudolph immediately turned to the stranger and asked him:

"Well, what do you think of the new novel?"

My heart lurched, and I squinted sideways at the young man's hands. They were holding the magazine open at my novel.

The young man became very animated and started talking in a gutteral voice.

"Rudolph Maximych! I just don't understand! You know best,

of course. But whatever made you print it, I simply can't understand. Apart from anything else, it isn't a novel at all."

"Then what is it?" asked Rudolph, enjoying my expression. His eyes were glowing.

"Damned if I know! Anyway, from my point of view, Rudolph Maximych, it's very poor, do forgive me! Totally untalented. And what's more he writes here "the roosters flew down". A rooster can't fly, R.M.! Tell the author that. He's untalented and illiterate into the bargain!"

"Tell him yourself," the bandit Rudolph replied. "Here he is. Let me introduce you. He says he went to a parish school."

I immediately got up and, baring my teeth in a smile, stretched out my hand to the young man. It was cold and lifeless. Pallid, he leaned back in his chair and said nothing while I took my free copies from Rudolph and departed.

On my way out I heard a thin wail:

"Rudolph Maximych!" and Rudolph's merry laughter.

My friend! You have probably read announcements like this: "The French writer X has written a novel. It sold out in France in a month, 600,000 copies, and has been translated into German, English, Italian, Swedish and Danish. In a month the ordinary clerk (or officer, or salesman, or station-master) has become world famous."

After a while you get hold of a dog-eared copy of some French or German illustrated magazine and see this favourite of the gods. He is wearing white trousers and a blue jacket. His hair is tousled, because a breeze is blowing from the sea. Beside him in a short and hat is an ugly woman with gorgeous teeth. She is holding a shaggy dog with pointed ears. You can see the side of the boat, a section of deck chair and some jagged waves in the distance. A caption says that the favoured one is happy and sailing off to America with his wife and dog.

Consumed by jealousy and grinding your teeth, you throw the magazine down on the table and light a cigarette. A foul stench rises from the ash-tray, long unemptied. The editorial office smells of boots and, for some reason, carbolic. The wet coats of the staff are hanging on hooks. It is autumn, but someone has come in a white-topped cap. It rots, sopping wet, on a nail. The rain is pouring down outside. It rained yesterday and it will rain again tomorrow too...

I shall not lie to you, my friend, my novel not only failed to come out in six hundred thousand copies, it failed to come out at all. As for the two-thirds of the novel that were published in Rudolph's magazine, they weren't translated into Danish, and I didn't sailed to America with my dog on a yacht. What is more, it produced so little impression that I began to think it hadn't come out at all. For about two months I didn't meet a soul who had read it. I myself, however, read what had been published at least fifteen times and came to the conclusion that Rudolph must have spirited the rough drafts away from my room one night. If I had worked on those drafts for another few months, I might have been able to make a decent novel out of them.

So two months went by. At the end of the second month I was finally persuaded that someone had read my work of art after all.

I happened to meet Vova Borguzin, the boozy, happy-go-lucky poet, at the editorial office. Vova said:

"I read your novel in the magazine. It's pretty weak, old boy..."

September 1929

Translated by Kate Cook

Elena Sergeyevna Bulgakova. 1937.

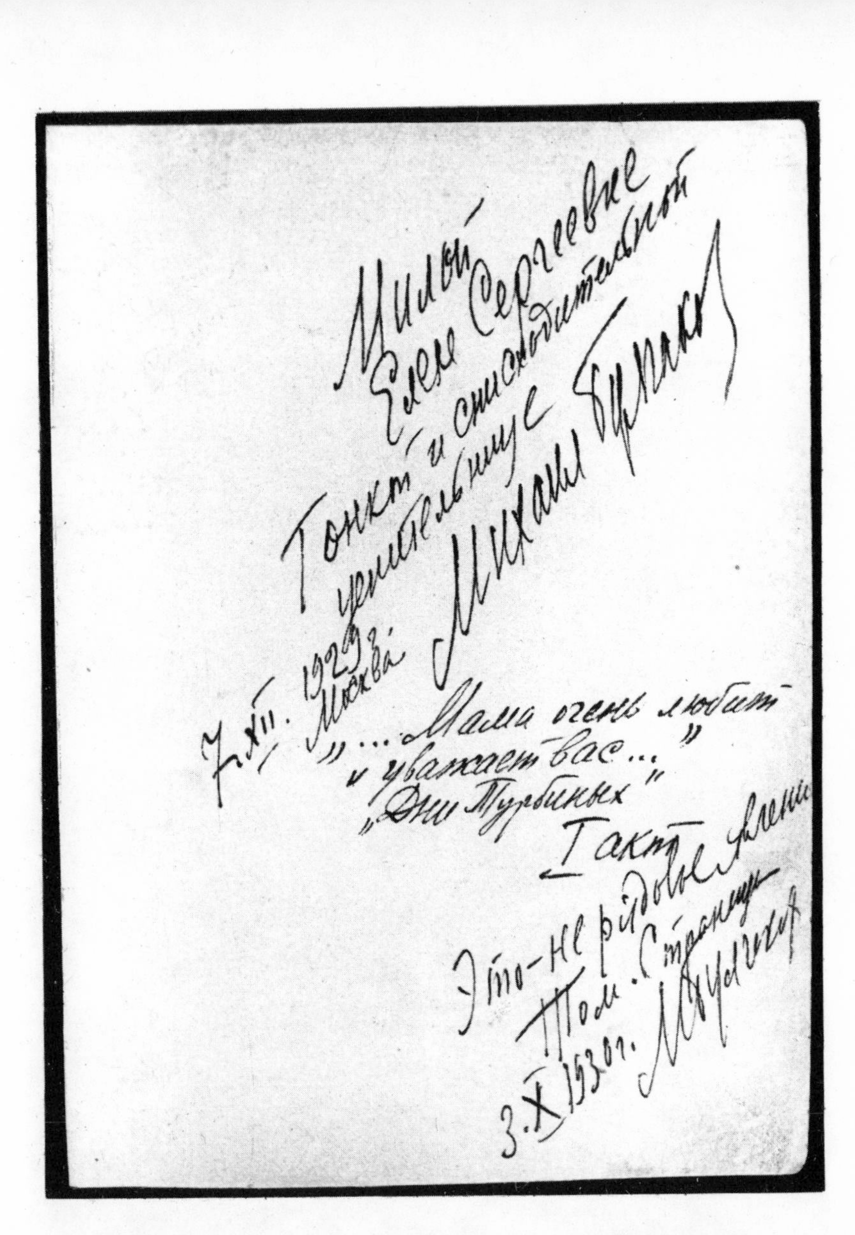

Милой Елене Сергеевне
Тонкой и снисходительной
ценительнице
Михаил Булгаков
7.XII.1929
Москва

„...Мама очень любит
и уважает вас..."
„Дни Турбиных"
I акт

Это — не рядовые явления
3.X.1930 г.

"To my dear Elena Sergeyevna, a subtle and benevolent critic..." "Mother loves and respects you..." — The Days of the Turbins, Act One. "These are no ordinary phenomena..."

Sinop, near Sukhumi in Abkhasia. 10 August 1936.

Elena Sergeyevna.

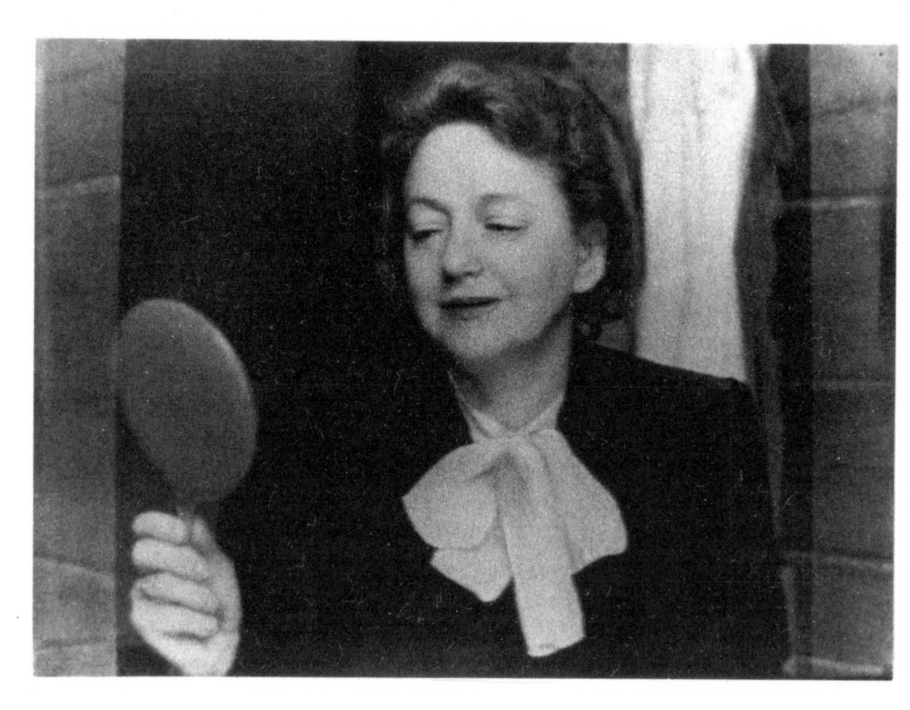

Elena Sergeyevna.

1934.Kiev.

"Their new home radiated happiness and wellbeing despite the hostility outside. Now he felt at every hour of the day that he was a writer and not a failure, a talented writer with an important work to do. and no right to doubt his calling. Everyday life became a source of happiness for him. "Praised be home!" he would write in his letters. The mistress of this home was irrepressibly light-hearted and full of energy and good will. Life was no longer terrifying." — from the memoirs of Sergei Yermolinsky, one of Bulgakov's close friends.

3. X. 38.

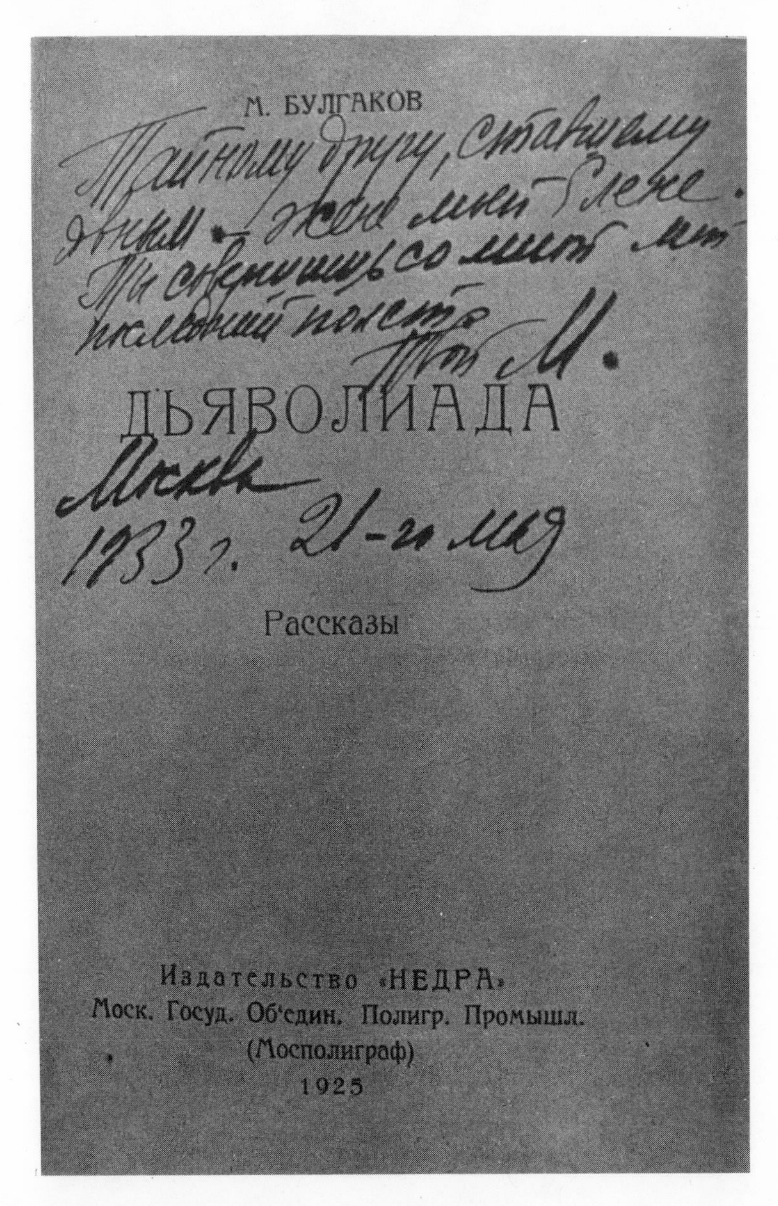

М. БУЛГАКОВ

ДЬЯВОЛИАДА

Рассказы

Издательство «НЕДРА»
Моск. Госуд. Об'един. Полигр. Промышл.
(Мосполиграф)
1925

"To my secret friend who has now come into the open. To my wife Elena. You will accompany me on my last flight." — May 24, 1933.
The title page of the "Diaboliad".

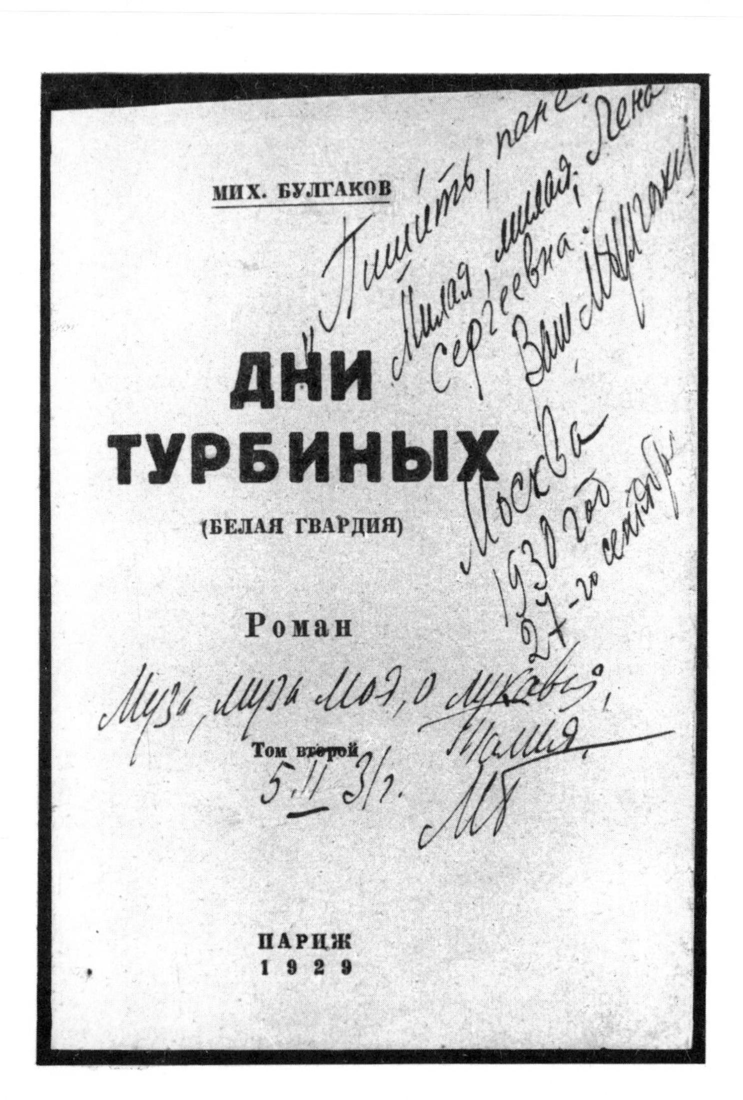

МИХ. БУЛГАКОВ

ДНИ ТУРБИНЫХ

(БЕЛАЯ ГВАРДИЯ)

Роман

Том второй

ПАРИЖ
1929

Пишите, пане!
Милая, милая Лена
Сергеевна!
Ваш М. Булгаков
Москва
1930 год
27-го сентября

Муза, муза моя, о лукавая
Талия.
5.II 31 г.
МБ

The title page of The Days of the Turbins. (The White Guard)
"Do write to me, my darling Elena Sergeyevna. Yours, Bulgakov". Moscow, 27 September 1930.
"My muse, my muse, my Thalia."

The late 1930s.

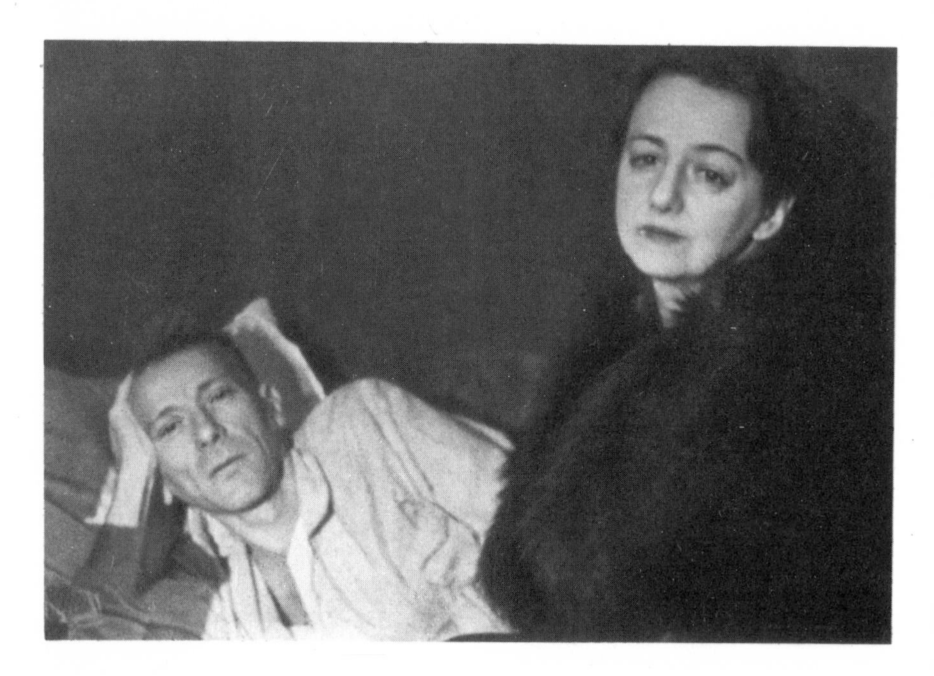

The last year of his life.

Bulgakov, Elena Sergeyevna, critic Popov, Sergei Shilovsky and M.Chimishkyan

Bulgakov with wife in 1939.

1940. "To my wife Elena Sergeyevna Bulgakova. This is for you alone, my friend and companion. Don't grieve because my eyes are dark. They've always been able to tell the truth from falsehood.
Moscow, Bulgakov, 11 February 1940."

1940. Elena Sergeyevna with actors of the Moscow Art Theatre.

The Diaries of Elena Sergeyevna

(Moscow, Knizhnaya Palata, 1991)
excerpts

These sketches were written down by Bulgakov's wife Elena Sergeyevna as he told them.

Fyodor Fyodorovich Raskolnikov*, at that time (round about 1929) director of the Repertoire Committee, wrote a play called *Robespierre*. He suggested to Nikitina that he read it at one of her Saturday Gatherings.

It was an unusually large meeting, several artistic directors were there, people like Bersenev and Tairov, and someone else whose name I have forgotten. The actors there were mostly sycophants.

Bulgakov seems to remember sitting in the furthest row by the central aisle.

Raskolnikov finished his reading and, after an extremely protracted ovation, said:

"Would anyone like to say anything now? Okay then, comrades, go ahead..."

This was said with a boss's swagger, and Bulgakov decided to say something, taking exception to his tone of voice. He raised his hand.

"Mr. Bersenev, Mr. Tairov..." the chairman of the meeting called out the names and wrote them down..." (I don't remember who the third was)... Bulgakov... (the man said in a slightly scared voice)... (and then came others who had raised their hands)".

Bersenev began.

"So comrades... we have just heard a marvellous creation by our dear Mr. Raskolnikov! (Several sycophants used this occasion to start

* Statesman and diplomat, admiral of the Navy, writer. In 1924-30, editor-in-chief of several magazines, later ambassador to Denmark and Bulgaria. Emigrated in 1938. — Ed.

applauding again). I'll be straight with you, and I'll be brief. I'd heard many superb plays in my time, but none that have had such an extraordinary effect on me, none that... I would say, have bowled me over, astounded me to this extent! I sat spellbound, quite lost for words... even now I'm finding it hard to speak, that's how excited I am! This is something special, comrades! We are witnessing something really special! I am choked for words! What can I say? Thank you, Mr. Raskolnikov, I am your humble servant! (And Bersenev bowed low to Raskolnikov, to the accompaniment of tempestuous applause from the audience.)

(Meanwhile Raskolnikov, with the words, "Okay then, comrades, go ahead", left the stage and sat in the third row, right in front of Bulgakov.)

"Who's next," said the chairman of the assembly. "Ah yes, esteemed Mr. Tairov!"

And Tairov began, slightly out of breath:

"Yes, comrades, it's not an easy task — assessing works like the one we have just been granted the honour of hearing! In my lifetime I have been to many discussions of plays by Shakespeare, Moliere, the classics such as Sophocles and Euripides... But comrades, these plays, despite the fact that they are, of course, masterpieces, are still somehow distant from us in time! (Murmur in the hall: this play isn't about modern times either!...) Right! It is not about contemporary times, but! Our dear Mr. Raskolnikov is truly masterful in his ability to take a non-contemporary theme and deal with it in such an unexpected way that it becomes extraordinarily close to our hearts, we actually seem to be living in the time of Robespierre, the time of the French Revolution! (Another murmur, but this time incomprehensible.) Comrades! Comrades! This is the sort of play that will give any theatre, any director the greatest pleasure to stage." (And Tairov, crossing his arms on his chest, then spreading them helplessly, went to his seat accompanied by even more tumultuous applause from the sycophants.)

Then a third speaker addressed the crowd:

"Of course I agree entirely with what the previous speakers have said in their high acclaim of the play by our esteemed Mr. Raskolnikov! I am only surprised that they failed to mention the most important thing in this superb piece of work! Language! In my time I have read many wonderful writers, and I both love and value the language of Turgenev and Tolstoy! But what we heard today left me speechless! What richness of language! What variety! What — I would even say — uniqueness! This play has a place among the classics of our literature on the merits of its rich language alone! Hooray!" (Someone seized on this and the audience burst into applause.)

"Whose turn is it now?" said the chairman. "Ah, comrade Bulgakov! Please."

Bulgakov got up, and without leaving his place began to speak, looking as he did at the neck of Raskolnikov, who, as we already know, was sitting in front of him.

"Hmm... I have been listening carefully to the previous speakers... very carefully... (Raskolnikov shuddered.) Mr. Bersenev said that in his whole life not a single play had moved him as much as this play by Raskolnikov. Well maybe., maybe... I'd just like to say that I feel truly sorry for Mr. Bersenev. After all he has worked in the theatre as an actor and director, and now as an artistic director, for many years. And now it turns out that all this time he has been working on material which leaves him cold. And only today... What a shame, what a shame... Similarly I didn't quite understand Mr. Tairov. He compared Raskolnikov's play to those of Shakespeare and Moliere. I am very fond of Moliere. And not only for the themes of his plays, or for the characters of his heroes, but also for his amazingly powerful dramatic technique. Every appearance by any character in Moliere's plays is necessary and to some purpose, and the intrigue develops in such a way that no link can be removed. In this play by Raskolnikov (Raskolnikov's neck went red), you can't understand what is going on, or why one particular character rather then another has come onto the stage. Or why he goes away again. The first act could be scrapped altogether, the second shifted to another place in the play... Like in an amateur performance!

"As for the language, I really pity the speaker who mentioned it, I pity him for the fact that he has never before today heard better language than in Raskolnikov's play. He spoke here about uniqueness. Yes, of course this language is unique... I'd just like to read out a few expressions I wrote down which particularly struck me... 'He imbibed this revolutionary ardour with his mother's milk'...

"Yes...

"What can I say, these things happen. The play's a failure."

The scene that followed, as Bulgakov told me later, resembled a bazaar where someone has just picked a fight.

There was sheer bedlam.

Subsequent speakers actually suggested getting rid of certain scenes and characters...

The meeting came to an end. "And now our dear Ivan Ivanovich will perform Chopin's Polonaise."The blood rushed to Raskolnikov's neck, it had gone dark blue.

Bulgakov got up and headed for the exit. Sensing a chill running down his spine, he turned round and saw Raskolnikov's eyes filled with hatred. His hand reached for his pocket. Bulgakov turned towards the door. "Is he going to shoot me in the back?"

* * *

In despair Bulgakov wrote a letter to Stalin, saying that he was writing plays but that no one would perform or print any of them, — just a short letter, very correctly written and signed: "Yours, Trampazlin."

Stalin receives the letter and reads it.

Stalin: What's this?... Tram-pa-zlin... What's that supposed to mean?

(Bulgakov always did Stalin's voice with a Georgian accent.)

Stalin (pressing a button on his desk): Get me Yagoda!*

Yagoda comes in, salutes.

Stalin: Listen, Yagoda, what is this? Look at this letter. It's written by some writer, and signed "Yours, Tram-pa-zlin". Who could that be?

Yagoda: I couldn't tell you.

Stalin: What d'you mean you couldn't tell me? How dare you answer me in that fashion? You should be able to see three fathoms under the ground! I want an answer in half an hour!

Yagoda: Yes, your excellency!

---

*The then Interior Minister

He leaves and comes back half an hour later.

Yagoda: So, your excellency, it seems it's Bulgakov!

Stalin: Bulgakov? What is the meaning of this? Why is my writer writing letters like that? Send for him immediately!

Yagoda: Yes, your excellency! (leaves.)

A motorcycle speeds down Furmanov Street — brrrrr!!! Brrrr!! There's a ring at the door and a man appears on our doorstep.

Man: Are you Bulgakov? My orders are to take you to the Kremlin immediately!

Bulgakov was wearing a pair of old white trousers. Shrunk in the wash, torn slippers with the toes showing through, and a creased shirt with a hole at the shoulder, and his hair was matted.

Bulgakov: Oh! Where can I... How can I... I've got no boots...

Man: I have to take you in whatever you're wearing, those are my orders!

Bulgakov takes off his slippers in terror and leaves with the man.

Errrr!!! goes the motorbike — and they're already in the Kremlin! Bulgakov is taken into a big room where he finds Stalin, Molotov, Voroshilov, Kaganovich, Mikoyan and Yagoda waiting for him.

Bulgakov stops in the doorway and takes a bow.

Stalin: What's this! Why are you barefoot?

Bulgakov: (throwing up his hands in despair). Well what can I do?... I've got no boots...

Stalin: What? My writer without boots? What a disgrace! Yagoda, take off your boots and give them to him!

Yagoda takes off his boots and gives them to Bulgakov in disgust. Bulgakov tries to put them on but they don't fit!

Bulgakov: They don't fit...

Stalin: What kind of feet have you got, Yagoda, I just don't understand! Voroshilov, take off your boots, perhaps yours are the right size.

Voroshilov takes off his boots, but they're too big for Bulgakov.

Stalin: Look, they're too big for him! That's quite a pair of legs you've got. Real army legs!

Voroshilov faints.

Stalin: This is no joke! Kaganovich, don't just sit there, can't you see this man has no boots!

(Kaganovich hurriedly takes off his boots, but they don't fit either.)

Well that's no surprise, he isn't Russian after all!.. Ohh.. just get out of my sight!

(Kaganovich faints.)

Never mind, he'll get over it! Mikoyan! Although there's no point in asking you, your legs are like a chicken's.

(Mikoyan staggers.)

Don't you dare fall! Molotov, take your boots off!

(Finally Molotov's boots fit.)

That's better. Great. Now tell me what's the matter with you? Why did you write me that letter?

Bulgakov: Well what is there to say... I keep writing plays, but what's the use!... At the moment, for instance, one of my plays is sitting somewhere in the Moscow Arts Theatre, but they won't stage it and they won't pay me for it...

Stalin: I see! Hold on a minute! Wait a second.

He makes a phone call.

Is that the Arts Theatre? This is Stalin. Get me Stanislavsky (Pause.) What? Died? When? Just now? (To Bulgakov.) Would you believe it, he died when they told him.

(Bulgakov sighs heavily.)

Hold on a moment, no need to sigh like that.

(He dials again.)

Is that the Arts Theatre? This is Stalin. Get me Nemirovich-Danchenko. (Pause) What? He's dead too? When... did he? Well, apparently he's died as well. Never mind, just a moment.

(He dials.)

Get me someone else then! Who's this? Yegorov? Right then, comrade Yegorov, you have in your theatre the manuscript of a play (nods to Bulgakov), a play by the writer Bulgakov... Of course I don't like to put pressure on people, but it seems to me that this is a good play... What? You think it's good too? And you're planning to stage it? And when do you think that will be? (He covers the receiver with his hand, and asks Bulgakov: "When do you want it?")

Bulgakov: Oh well! In three years or so would do!

Stalin: Hmmm!... (To Yegorov) I don't like to interfere in

theatrical matters, but it seems to me that you (winks at Bulgakov) could stage it in... three months or so... What? In three weeks? Good, good. And how much were you thinking of paying him for it?... (He covers the receiver with his hand and asks Bulgakov: "How much do you want?")

Bulgakov: We-ell... I'd say... about 500 roubles would be okay!

Stalin: Ohh!... (To Yegorov.) Of course I'm not a specialist in financial matters, but it seems to me that you ought to pay about fifty thousand for a play like that. What? Sixty? Okay then! (To Bulgakov.) Well there you are, you see, and you said...

* * *

After that Stalin simply can't live without Bulgakov — they're together all the time. But one day Bulgakov comes and says:

Bulgakov: I need to go to Kiev for three weeks or so.

Stalin: And you call yourself a friend? What about me?

But Bulgakov went all the same, And Stalin was left to pine away all on his own.

"Oh my Misha, my Misha!.. He's gone, he's left me! What am I to do, I'm so terribly bored!... Maybe I should go to the theatre?.. Zhdanov keeps going on about Soviet music... We must go to the opera."

He starts phoning everyone up.

"Is that Voroshilov? What are you up to? You're working? Well what you do is pointless anyway. Careful, don't faint! Come over, we're going to the opera. Bring Budyonny with you!"

"Hallo, Molotov, come over right now, we're going to the opera! What? You're stammering so much I can't understand you! Come over, I said! And bring Mikoyan with you!"

"Hallo, Kaganovich, stop acting the Jew and get over here, we're going to the opera."

"Right then, Yagoda, you must have been listening in to all that, so you know we're going to the opera. Get the car ready!"

The car was driven up, and they all got in. At the last moment Stalin remembered:

Stalin: How could we have forgotten the great art expert?

We've forgotten Zhdanov! Send the fastest aeroplane to fetch him from Leningrad!

Brrr!.. The aeroplane soars into the air and a few minutes later comes back with Zhdanov.

Stalin: Wow that was quick! We thought we'd go to the opera, what with you going on about the flourishing State of Soviet music! Well now you can show us! Get in. Oh, there's no room? Well sit on my lap then, you're small enough.

The car goes brrr.. and they all go into the government box at the Bolshoi.

Meanwhile in the theatre everyone's in a wild panic, they know the great man is coming. Yakov L. has phoned Shostakovich and artistic director Samosud, who's got tonsilitis. In five minutes Samosud arrives at the theatre — his throat is bandaged up and he has a temperature. Shostakovich, white with fear, also makes a rapid entry. Melik, wearing a dinner jacket with a red carnation in his buttonhole, prepares to conduct the orchestra for the second performance of Shostakovich's *Lady Macbeth*. Everyone is anxious, but on the whole pleasantly so, because not long before this the boss and his retinue had gone to see *Quiet Flows the Don*, and on the following day all the performers were awarded medals and titles. So today all of them, — Samosud, Shostakovich and Melik — are picking holes in the left side of their jackets.

The occupants of the government box take their places. Melik waves his baton fiercely and begins the overture. In anticipation of a medal, and sensing the eyes of all the leaders upon him, Melik rages, jumps around, cuts through the air with his baton and sings silently to the orchestra. The sweat pours off him thick and fast. "Never mind, in the interval I'll change my shirt", he thinks ecstatically.

After the overture he looks sideways at the government box, expecting applause, but there is none, not a stir.

After the first act the same thing happens, they are unimpressed. Opposite — in the theatre's private box — stand Samosud, with a towel round his neck, Shostakovich, shaking, and the magnificently calm Yakov Leontyev, deputy director of the Bolshoi, — he has nothing to lose. Straining their necks they look anxiously at the government box, where there is total calm.

This goes on right through the performance. Nobody thinks about medals any more. It's more a question of staying alive...

When the opera ends, Stalin gets up and says to his entourage:

"I would ask you comrades to stay behind. Let's go outside, we need to talk."

They go outside.

"Right then, comrades, we need to have a collective discussion. (They all sit down.) Now I don't like to put pressure on people, I'm not going to say that in my opinion this opera is a cacophony or a musical muddle, instead let me ask my comrades to express their opinions absolutely independently."

Stalin: Voroshilov, you're the oldest, tell me what you think about this music?

Voroshilov: Well actually, yourness, I think it's a muddle.

Stalin: Sit down beside me, Klim, sit down. Molotov, what do you think?

Molotov: I, y-your e-excellency, th-think it's a c-cacophony.

Stalin: Okay okay, that's enough of your stammering! Sit here next to Klim. Well what does our Zionist think of it all?

Kaganovich: Well I think that it's a cacophony and a muddle as well!

Stalin: I won't ask Mikoyan, all he knows about is tinned food... Now now, no need to collapse! Budyonny, what do you say?

Budyonny (stroking his moustache): They should all get the chop!

Stalin: What, you mean just like that? You're a fierce one! Sit closer! So, comrades, you've all given your opinions and reached a consensus. The collective meeting has gone well. Let's go home.

They all get into the car. Zhdanov is bewildered because his opinion wasn't asked for, and he rolls around at everyone's feet.

He tries to sit in his old place, on Stalin's lap.

Stalin: Where do you think you're going? Are you out of your mind? On the way here you made my legs numb! Soviet music!... Flourishing state!... You can walk home!

The next morning the newspaper *Pravda* carried the article:

"A Musical Muddle". In it the word "cacophony" was repeated several times.

From Elena Sergeyevna's letter to her brother Alexander Nurenberg.

...In a few days there will be another anniversary — 32 years since the day I met Misha. It was on Shrove Tuesday, at the house of some mutual acquaintances. They urged me to come along saying that the famous Bulgakov would be there, and I agreed immediately. I was already very keen on his writing. They had enticed him, by saying that some interesting people would be there — in a word, he came.

We happened to sit beside each other (my husband was away on business and I was alone). Some lace had fallen loose on my sleeve and I asked him to fasten it. He always believed afterwards that this had been a piece of sorcery, that I had fastened him to myself for life. What he liked most of all, of course, was that I hung on his every word, waiting for another shaft of wit. Aware that he had such a receptive audience, he unwound completely, and gave such a performance that he had everyone groaning with laughter. He leapt up from the table, played the piano, sang, danced, in short he put on a show. His eyes were bright blue, and when he let himself go like this, they sparkled like diamonds.

We agreed to go skiing next day. And we did. After skiing, we went to the dress rehearsal of "The Siege" — then to the Actors' Club, where he played billiards with Mayakovsky. I hated Mayakovsky and so patently wanted him to lose that he said he was scarcely able to hold his cue. (He played a more even game than Misha, who was sometimes brilliant and sometimes missed his shots completely). We began to meet every day, until at last I begged Misha for a rest, saying I wouldn't go out anywhere, that I wanted an early night, that he should not call me that day.

I went to bed early, just after nine o'clock. That night (it was about three, I found out later), our housekeeper Olenka who did not approve of any of this, of course, woke me — "Your Mr. Bulgakov's on the phone." (She was very annoyed.) I went to the phone — "Get dressed and come out to the front steps", said Misha enigmatically, and with no explanation just repeated his words.

He was living at this time on Bolshaya Pirogovskaya Street,

while we were on the Sadovaya, on the corner of Malaya Bronnaya Street, in a house old enough to have seen Napoleon, with open fireplaces, a semi-basement kitchen, round windows that seemed filmed with radiance — but never mind all that, what mattered was that we lived a long way from each other.

He repeated "Come out to the front steps." Accompanied by Olenka's grumbling, I got dressed (my husband was still away) and went out. Misha stood all white in the brilliant moonlight, on the steps. He took my hand and, to all my questions and laughter, he only put his finger to his lips and kept silent. He led me along the street, as far as the Patriarch's Ponds, to a particular tree, and said, pointing to a bench: "This is where they saw him for the first time." And again — his finger to his lips; again, silence.

Then he led me on, still holding my hand, to some house near the Ponds, took me up to the second floor, and rang the bell. An old man came to the door, very grand, very tall, handsome, with a luxuriant beard, in a tight-fitting white coat and high boots. Then a young man appeared, his son. We all went into the dining room. A fire was burning in the grate, and on the table there was fish-soup, caviare, other delicacies and wine. We had a veritable feast and a lot of fun.

From his conversation I understood that the old man had been a wholesaler in fish and fish-products, had been exiled and returned to his son in Moscow (he was from Astrakhan himself). He had brought with him all this fish, given him by old friends in Astrakhan. We sat until morning. I was sitting on the carpet when the old man suddenly said, "May I kiss you?" "You may, you may kiss me on the cheek." And he said, "A witch, a witch! You have cast a spell over me!" "I understood then", Misha used to say later, happily remembering that evening, or night, rather, "that you are a witch! You enchanted me!"

We went home, and I still have no idea where we went that night. Misha never mentioned the old man's surname, and always assured me that I had dreamed it all. Maybe he wasn't a fish merchant, may be was not from Astrakhanat all and had never been exiled, and it was all an elaborate practical joke? I don't know. Misha loved to play practical jokes.

From Bulgakov's letter to V.Veresayev dated 11 July 1934.

"On May 17th I was lying on the sofa. A phone call, a stranger, some official, I suppose. "You've put in your application? Go to the Foreign Department of the Moscow Executive Committee and fill in the questionnaires, you and your wife."

By about four o'clock in the afternoon we had filled in the forms. The official said: "You will receive your passports very shortly, there's a special instruction about your case. You could have had them today if you'd come a bit earlier. You will receive them on the 19th."

Tsvetnoy Boulevard, sunshine, Elena Sergeyevna and I walked all the way to the centre, talking of only one thing — could that be true or we dreamed it all? I don't usually suffer from auditory hallucinations, and neither does she.

One of the reasons I had given for my journey was that I wanted to write a book about my travels in Western Europe.

The atmosphere at home was blissful. Can you imagine? — Paris — Moliere's statue — Hallo, M. de Moliere, I have written a book and a play about you! Hallo, Mr. Gogol, don't be angry, I have turned your "Dead Souls" into a play. True, it's not exactly like the one that's been staged, not like it all, but it's my work nevertheless... The Mediterranean! Oh heavens!

Would you believe it, I've begun to plan the chapters of the book.

So many of our writers have been to Europe — and they've all come back empty-handed! Nothing! I think, if we sent our Sergey to Europe, he could tell us more interesting stories than them. Maybe I shall not be able to, either. Forgive me, but I shall try! On the 19th, no passports. On the 23rd, they said they'd be ready on the 25th. On the 25th, ready on the 27th. We get worried. We asked, was there really a special instruction? Yes, there was. Through the Arts Theatre, we learned that, according to the Government Commission, "The Bulgakov matter is settled."

What more do they need? Nothing.

We must wait patiently. So we do.

Now we have started to say our goodbyes. A little envy, "Oh, you lucky people!"

"Wait", I say, "where are our passports?"

"Don't worry!" (in chorus).

So we don't worry. Dreams. Rome, a balcony, like me one Gogol used to write about.. Pines, roses...drawings... I'll dictate to Elena Sergeyevna... in the evenings we'll take a walk, it will be quiet, full of sweet scents... In a word, a novel! In September I grow uneasy. Kamergersky Lane* — there will be showers, the stage will be dark, back-stage they're probably getting "Moliere" ready.

And then, out of the showers, I appear. Manuscript in my suitcase. There you are!

Our Moscow Arts folk are the most sober on earth. They don't believe in roses or showers. Imagine it, they believe that Bulgakov should go abroad. That's serious! They even believe that the Moscow Arts list of passport recipients (and this year there are a lot of them) will include me and Elena Sergeyevna. They gave the list to the messenger — "go and get the passports", they said.

He went, and he came back. His expression filled me with such displeasure that my heart sank at once, before he had opened his mouth.

To be brief, he brought passports for everybody, but for me, a blank sheet of paper — M. A. Bulgakov, refused.

There wasn't even a sheet of paper for Elena Sergeyevna. Well, we won't even talk about her!

My impression of all this? By all the saints of Russian literature, I swear it was grandiose! I could best describe it as the derailment of an express train. A well-appointed, well-equipped train, with the lights green, on the rails, — and suddenly bang! It's lying at the bottom of the embankment.

I emerged from the wreckage, not a pretty sight!"

From Elena Sergeyevna's letters to Bulgakov's brother Nikolai:

...He used to destroy all his manuscripts before we met, and only the type-written copies remained. But since 1930 I have kept

*The location of the Moscow Arts Theatre

every page, every line. Misha used to laugh at me to begin with, but then he began to help me, and never threw anything away.

Everyone thought Misha had calmed down, that, if I can put it this way, he had brightened up outwardly. By 1939 he had become quite charming, in both body and spirit. Even with all his habitual talk about his impending death (he always spoke about this in the most amusing way, at the dinner table with friends, where everyone was reduced to laughter by his play-acting and his brilliant conversation).

Since he was always returning to this subject, I would insist once a year on his having all sorts of tests and X-rays. The results were always all right, and the only thing that bothered him was headaches — and he kept these at bay with painkillers. But in the autumn of 1939 he was suddenly taken ill and suffered a momentary loss of eyesight (this was in Leningrad, where we had gone for a holiday), and the professor who examined him said: "This is serious. You must go home." This brutality on the doctor's part was repeated in Moscow — they gave him no hope, saying: "You are a doctor yourself, you must understand."

From the first days when Misha asked me to live with him, he made me swear never to let him be taken to hospital, but to let him die in my arms, saying that he wanted it to be the same as with his father, Afanassy Ivanovich. He even foretold the year — 1939. The doctors told me as well, that it was a matter of only three or four days. But Misha lived on after this for another seven months, "because", as he said, "I believe in you."

...For a long time I did nothing to decorate the grave; I just planted flowers all over it, and four pear saplings round it, which have grown into wonderfully tall trees, making an arch of green over the grave. I could not find anything that I wanted to see on the grave, nothing worthy of him. Then one day, when I was paying one of my frequent visits to the monumental masonry near the Novodevichy Cemetery, I saw a block of granite hidden away in a hole. The manager, when I asked him, explained it was the Golgotha from Gogol's tomb, discarded when they built a new memorial for him. At my request, and with the help of an excavator, they hauled out this stone, transported it to Misha's grave, and erected it there. With great difficulty, for the granite was hard to work, like steel, the workmen cut a plaque for the inscription: "Mikhail Afanassievich Bulgakov, writer: 1891—1940" (Four lines. Gold lettering.) You will appreciate how appropriate this is for Misha's grave — the Golgotha from the tomb of his beloved Gogol. Now, every spring, I just plant some grass. There is a thick emerald carpet, and on it the Golgotha stone, and above it all a dome of thick green branches. It is marvellously beautiful and original, as everything about Misha was original, both the man and the artist... It would be impossible to inscribe the verses you suggest (the idea is wonderful and suitable) because, as I said, it's so hard to inscribe this granite, even more so if the print is fine. It is a block of Black Sea granite, which Aksakov brought especially for Gogol's tomb.

Now I want to describe Misha's death to you in more detail, however painful it is for me. I understand that you have to know this. When Misha and I realised that we could not live without each other (that is exactly how he expressed it), he added suddenly, very seriously, "please understand that I shall be dying in great pain. Give me your word that you won't send me to hospital, but let me die here in your arms." I smiled, unintentionally — this was in 1932. Misha was a little over forty, in good health, still young... He repeated, with great seriousness, "Give me your word." Afterwards during our life together he sometimes reminded me of my promise.

I used to insist that he should visit his doctor, have X-rays, tests and so forth. He did all this, and everything was fine, but nonetheless he had named 1939 as the year of his death, and when that year came, he began to say, in a light, joking tone, that this was now the last year, the last play, and so on. But since his health continued to prove excellent, you couldn't take what he said seriously. He always talked about this after dinner, with friends, in his inimitable brilliant manner, with lucid good humour, so that everyone became used to this topic. Then we went south for the summer, and he was taken ill in the train. The doctors explained to me later that this had been a mild stroke. This was on August 15th, 1939. We returned the same day from Tula, where I found a car to take us to Moscow. I called the doctor; Misha stayed in bed for a short time, then got up, but grew depressed, and we decided to go to Leningrad for a while, for a change of surroundings. We left on September 10th, but returned after four days, because on our first outing on Nevski Prospekt, he felt as though he were going blind. We found a professor there, who said after examining Misha's eyes: "This is serious." He insisted that I should take Misha home at once. In Moscow I called the most eminent professors, eye and kidney specialists. The first wanted to take Misha away with him at once to the Kremlin Hospital. But Misha said: "I shall never leave her." And he reminded me of my oath.

When I was saying goodbye to Professor Vovsy in the hall, he said: "I don't insist, it's only a matter of three days." But Misha lived for another six months. Sometimes he was better, sometimes worse. Sometimes he even went out, to the theatre. But he slowly grew weaker and thinner, and his sight deteriorated. We usually went to bed after one in the morning, and after an hour or two he would awaken me and say, "Get up, Lyusenka, I'm going to die soon. Let's talk." It is true that after a moment he would be cracking jokes and laughing, and believing me, when I said he would soon recover, and inventing unlikely satirical articles about the Moscow Arts Theatre, or the reading of a new novel, all sorts of funny things. Then, much calmer, he would go back to sleep. As a doctor, he knew everything that was going to happen, asked for tests to be done; sometimes I managed to fake these, when his albumen level was too high.

There was an unending stream of visitors — friends, acquaintances, strangers. Towards the end, many of them stayed overnight, sleeping on the floor. My son Zhenya stopped going to school and stayed with me to help me through the impending horror. Elena too was often with us; the painters V. Dimitriev and B. Erdman (both dead now) came every day. The Yermolinskys (close friends) lived with us. The nurses were there continuously, and the doctors followed every change in Misha's condition. But it was all in vain. His strength left him, it took two or three men to lift him every day when his sheets were changed. He had lost the use of his legs. My place was a cushion on the floor by his bed. He held my hand all this time, until the last second.

On the 9th March the doctor said, at about three in the afternoon, that he had two hours to live, not more. Misha was lying as though unconscious. The night before, he had been suffering terribly, everything hurt. He asked for my son Seryozha to be called, and placed his hand on his head. He cried: "Light!" and all the lamps were switched on.

On the 9th, a few hours after the doctor had passed sentence, he regained consciousness, and drew me to him. I leaned down to kiss him. He held me for so long, it seemed an eternity. His breath was cold as ice. The final kiss. On the morning of the 10th he was still asleep (or unconscious), and his breathing was faster, warmer, more even. I suddenly had this crazy conviction that the miracle I had always promised him, and I had made him to believe, was actually happening — that he would recover, that this was the crisis.

When at about three o'clock Leontyev called (he was the Director of the Bolshoi Theatre — our great friend, now dead), I said to him, "Look, Misha is getting better! Do you see?" And it seemed to me and to Leontyev that there was a slight smile on Misha's face. Perhaps it was only an illusion. But perhaps he heard us?

After a while I left the room, when suddenly my son Zhenya ran after me. "Mummy, he's looking for your hand," I ran back, took his hand, and Misha began to breathe faster and faster, then unexpectedly opened his eyes wide and sighed. His eyes were filled with amazement and some strange light. He was dead.

It was 4.39 in the afternoon, I noted it in my diary. During his illness I began by writing down the doctor's prescriptions, then added a complete account of each day, what medicines he took and when, what he ate, when and how long he slept. Then, his words. Later, when his condition deteriorated, the distraught moments when he lost his memory (very rare), his hallucinations, and finally detailed notes of the last days of his suffering. His face had altered so much from all the pain he had borne, that he had become almost unrecognizable. I thought with horror — I shall never see Misha again as I knew him. But after his death, his face was peaceful, almost happy, young. There was a slight smile on his lips. I was not alone in seeing this: everyone who saw him spoke of it with wonder.

On 4th March I was awakened by the nurse, saying, "Mikhail Afanassievich is asking for you, he wants to say goodbye." I went to him. He looked askance at the nurse, waiting for her to have the sense to leave, but she went over to the window, and did not go. In jest, he made as if to spit at her, just lightly and silently — this always made me laugh. Then, suddenly serious, he spoke his last words of farewell, words he had never before used, even to me who had listened to him for so long. He collapsed after this, and fell back on his pillow, growing cold and his face turning blue before my eyes. I cradled his head in my arms, and began convulsively to talk to him, about how we would soon be off to Italy, how he would get better there, how good it would be on the train, how the wind would blow the curtains... And he began to revive, and murmured, "More, more about the curtains, about the wind."

When the doctor came that evening, Misha said: "You know, Nikolay Antonovich, I died today, in her arms, but I have risen again."

He died as manfully as he had lived. You were right when you said that few people would have chosen the path he did. With his undoubted talents he could have lived a very easy life and won recognition everywhere. He could have enjoyed all life's blessings. But he was a true artist — upright and honest. He could only write about what he believed in. Everyone who knew him, or knew at least his work, had an immense admiration for him. For many people, he was their conscience. For all who came into contact with him, he was irreplaceable.

Translated by James Escomb

Bulgakov and Elena Sergeyevna are buried together.

Elena Sergeyevna

"My little queen" this was the dying Bulgakov's affectionate nickname for his wife Elena Sergeyevna. It was she who made it possible for him to complete his magnum opus, *The Master and Margarita*, and have a measure of human happiness during those horrible years of the totalitarian regime when so many intellectuals paid with their lives for any lack of conformism.

Since the day they married in the autumn of 1932 Elena Sergeyevna and Mikhail Bulgakov were hardly ever separated.

She was closer to him than anybody, she suffered through all his projects, his accomplishments, hardships and disasters as though they were her own.

When Elena Sergeyevna moved in with Bulgakov, he told her, "The whole world has been against me, and I have been alone. Now we are two, and I fear nothing."

Elena Sergeyevna: "I was young, and had just got to know Bulgakov, at the time when he was being torn to pieces over *The White Guard* and *The Days of the Turbins.* I asked him: "But why don't you write a play about the Red Army instead of the Whites?" He fixed me with an intense stare and said, deeply offended: "As you seem not to understand, I should love to write such a play, but I cannot write about what I do not know.""

From 1933 to the day of Bulgakov's death in March 1940 Elena Sergeyevna kept a diary recording every day's events (published by Knizhnaya Palata, Moscow, 1991), and for thirty years afterwards she consistently promoted Bulgakov's work in an effort to get it published.

Despite the literary authorities' general lack of interest in Bulgakov in those years and, consequently, his inaccessibility to the general public, she had complete confidence in her husband's genius. Bulgakov's plays were slanderously reviewed in the press and promptly banned by the censor. They lived in squalor, aware that his works will have a long life... in his desk drawer.

Elena Sergeyevna was Bulgakov's third wife. She left her first husband, General Shilovsky, to go and live with Bulgakov in a communal flat. "Love sprang out like a killer from around a corner," said Bulgakov in *The Master and Margarita* describing what happened to them both. Despite the poverty and persecution they were blissfully happy together. They had a narrow circle of friends who were the only readers of his unpublished works at that time. When he lost his sight she took down his dictation of *The Master and Margarita* and she swore to him that she would get the book published. She kept her word.

She religiously preserved all of Bulgakov's papers, every single scrap of paper. At the point where their life together came to an end, another period opened for her, during which his letters, and everything else he had written and she had retained, must be handed on to literature. She considered Bulgakov a great writer, and her belief in his genius was a part of her life, of her love for him.

In his letters Bulgakov longs to be reunited with his wife "I've grown accustomed to sharing my burden with you"... "My wish is to converse with you alone!" "Oh Koo, from where you are, so far away, you cannot see what the last sunset novel of your husband has done to him after his dreadful life in literature"...

She was convinced that his letters, sooner or later, should reach the readers, and did everything to ensure this. She kept them in perfect order — 64 registered letters, postcards and telegrams. She kept the envelopes together with the letters. On each telegram she wrote with a light yellow felt pen (that would not divert the eye) the date and year in the lower left-hand corner. (on telegrams, then as now, the year of despatch is not shown, and researchers know only too well how this can complicate their work). She erased with India ink all passages that, in her view, related only to her. She destroyed her replies. Not long before her death, she transferred these letters, together with all the rest of the archives in her possession, to the safekeeping of the State — to the Manuscript Department of the Lenin Library in Moscow.

In 1946, through a fashionable dressmaker in a government salon, she managed to get a letter to A.N.Poskryobishev for Stalin. Poskryobishev telephoned her a month later. "Your letter has been read. Call Chagin (director of the State Publishing House) in two or three weeks, he will be au courant...". "I didn't walk during those days, I flew." Elena Sergeyevna lived through those two or three weeks somehow, and then the newspaper published the resolution banning Akhmatova and Zoshchenko. "I realised that it was all over. I phoned for form's sake and received the reply, "It's not the right moment."

Only at the seventh or eighth attempt was she successful in getting *The Master and Margarita* published. How she rejoiced then, how lovingly she stroked the lilac-coloured leaves of the journal *Moskva*!

In 1970, when a collection of Bulgakov's major novels: *The White Guard*, *The Master and Margarita* and *Theatrical Novel*, was sent to the printers, she said joyfully:"Now I can die in peace." And indeed the summer of 1970 was her last. She died suddenly of heart failure.

Many contemporaries observed that Elena Sergeyevna had the power to draw people like a magnet. She inspired complete trust in people and enchanted everyone. The famous translator Michael Glenny, the first to introduce *The Master and Margarita* to the English-reading public, recalls the impression she made on him: "I doubt if at any time in my life I have experienced so much goodness, warmth and kindness... It would be an understatement to say that there are few people in this world like Elena Sergeyevna. Rather, she was unique, irreplaceable, in the most profound meaning of the word."

Among her close friends were such people as Anna Akhmatova who dedicated a poem to her. They had a great spiritual closeness and Akhmatova often felt the need to discuss her innermost feelings with Elena Sergeyevna alone. Akhmatova admired and respected Elena Sergeyevna's loyal dedication to her mission of bringing Bulgakov's work to the attention of the reading public. Elena Sergeyevna was also a great friend of Svyatoslav Richter, the famous pianist, who spent much time with her. She was indispensible to him. When asked about her he said:"Read *The Master and Margarita* and you'll know all there is to know about her."

It is only thanks to her courage, determination and love that we can enjoy the work of this great Russian writer today.

Bulgakov's books available in English translations

The Days of the Turbins, in: *An Anthology of Russian Plays*, tr. F.D.Reeve, 1963.

The Adventures of Chichikov, tr. Lydia W. Kesich, in: *Great Soviet Short Stories*, ed. by F.D.Reeve

The Fatal Eggs, tr. Mirra Ginsburg.

The Master and Margarita, tr. Michael Glenny, Harvill, UK, and Harper and Row, US, 1967.

Black Snow: Theatrical Novel, tr Michael Glenny, Harvill, 1986.

The Heart of a Dog, tr. Michael Glenny, Harvill, 1968.

The White Guard, tr. Michael Glenny, Harvill, 1971.

A Country Doctor's Notebook, tr Michael Glenny, Harvill, 1975, 1992.

Diaboliad, tr. Carl Proffer, Harvill, 1991.

Books about Bulgakov (in English)

Lesley Milne, *The Master and Margarita: A Comedy of Victory*, Birmingham University Slavonic Monographs series, 1977.

A.Colin Wright, *Mikhail Bulgakov: Life and Interpretations*, University of Toronto Press, 1978.

Ellendea Proffer, *Bulgakov: Life and Work*, Ardis, Ann Arbor, 1984.

Kalpana Sahni, *A Mind in Ferment: Mikhail Bulgakov's Prose*, Arnold Heinemann, New Delhi, 1984.

Julie Curtis, *Bulgakov's Last Decade: The Writer as Hero*, Cambridge University Press, 1987.

Andrew Barratt, *Between Two Worlds:"The Master and Margarita"*, Clarendon Press, Oxford, 1987.

Manuscripts don't Burn. A Life in Diaries and Letters. Harvill, 1992.

Osip MANDELSTAM

/1891 – 1938/

Emily Veniaminovich Mandelstam, the poet's father. 1890s.
(Evgeny Mandelstam's archives)

Flora Osipovna Verblovskaya, the poet's mother. 1890s.
(Evgeny Mandelstam's archives)

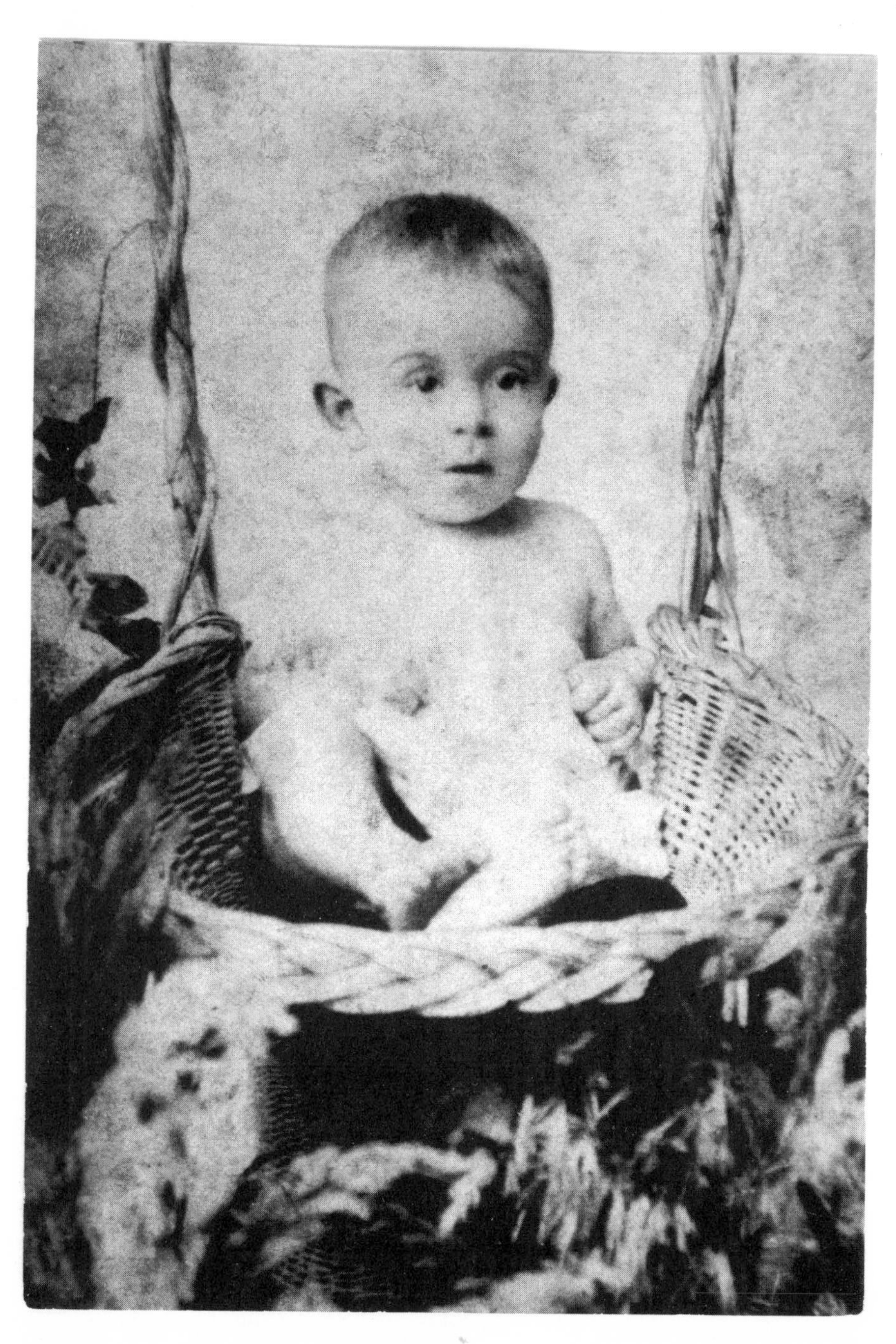

Osip Mandelstam. 1891. (Yuri Freidin's collection)

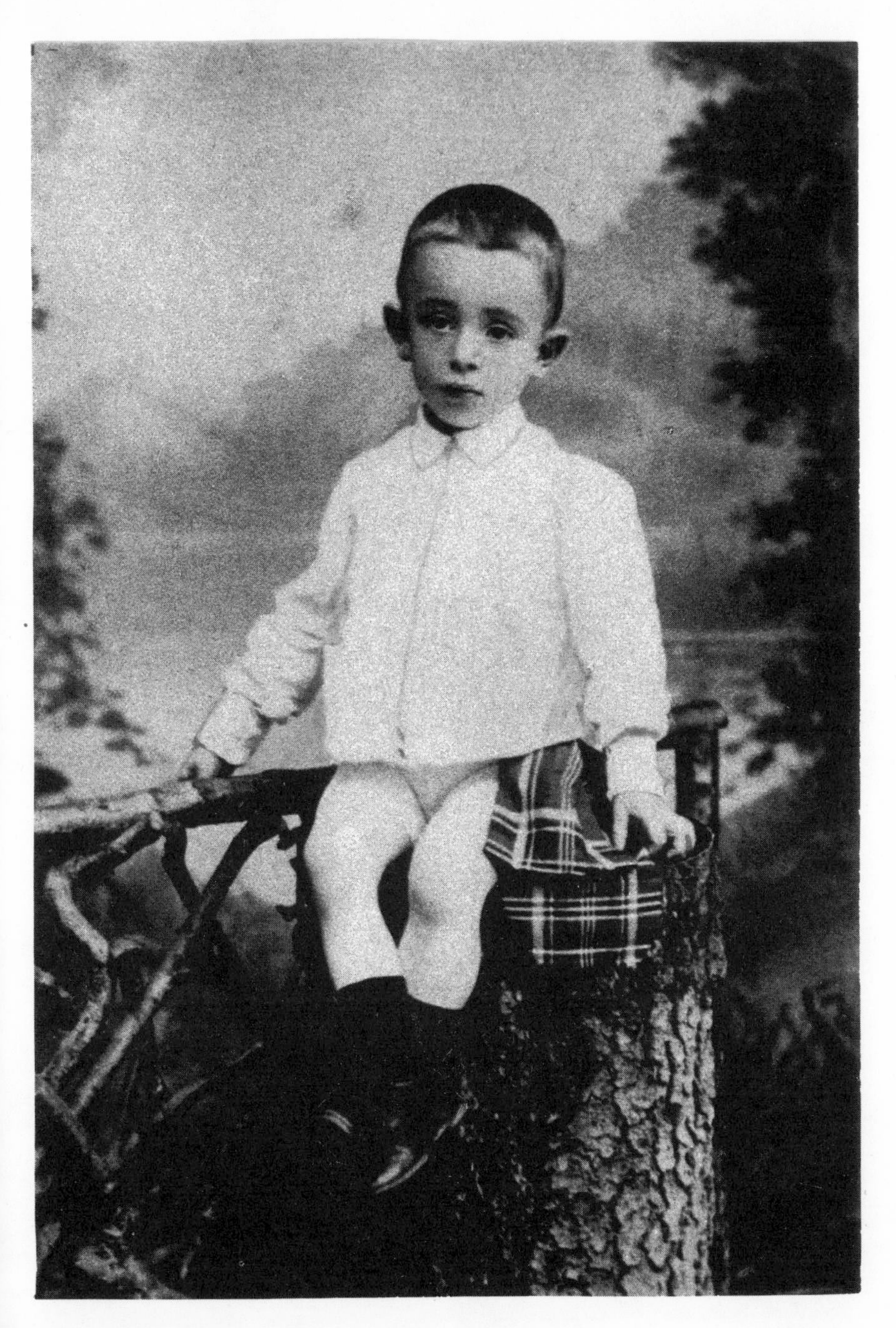

Osip Mandelstam. 1894. (Evgeny Mandelstam's archives)

Osip and Alexander Mandelstam. 1897.
(Evgeny Mandelstam's archives)

Osip and Alexander Mandelstam. 1899.
(Evgeny Mandelstam's archives)

Osip Mandelstam. 1906.
(Evgeny Mandelstam's archives)

Osip Mandelstam. 1908. Paris.
(Evgeny Mandelstam's archives)

Osip Mandelstam. 1912. Vyborg (Finland).
(Yuri Freidin's collection)

Osip Mandelstam. 1913.
(Yuri Freidin's collection)

"Crazy Ship", a pen drawing by N. Radlov (1920s), (from left to right: Georgy Ivanov, Nikolai Gumilev, Vladimir Khodasevich, Vyacheslav Shishkov, Viktor Shklovsky, Alexei Remizov, Osip Mandelstam, A.Volynsky), a metaphor for the Petrograd "Arts Club" frequented by the intelligentsia in the city devastated by the Civil War. Here Mandelstam used to come in the winter of 1920-21. (SLM)

Osip Mandelstam. 1913.
(State Literature Museum)
A drawing by E. Kruglikova

О. МАНДЕЛЬШТАМЪ.

КАМЕНЬ

СТИХИ.

АКМЭ.

С.-ПЕТЕРБУРГЪ

1913.

SILENTIUM

It's still not clear when she'll be born,
For now — is heard both word and music,
A seal best when left unbroken
Else fastened shells would be forlorn.

See ocean's bosom gently heaving,
And there's distracted, bright-faced day,
With palest lilac boughs of spray,
Atop dark-azure vessel, breathing.

But should my lips toward her approach
To find in destiny a dumbness, —
A tone so crystal as a sea sol, —
Whose virgin self my breath does broach!

Remain as foam, O Aphrodite, —
And, word, restore your music's link, —
And heart's pursuit of heart, rethink, —
For here combine the sounds of Oneness!
1910

Translated by Eric Guth

The front cover of Mandelstam's first poetic collection, *Stone*. (SLM)

Anna Akhmatova. 1915. (SLM)

Nikolai Gumilev.
In 1912, Gumilev, Akhmatova, Mandelstam, and several other poets founded a literary group called "acmeists" in opposition to Symbolists. (SLM)

Osip Mandelstam, Korney Chukovsky, Benedikt Liefshitz and Yuri Annenkov. Petrograd. 1914.
Poet Benedikt Liefshitz had been drafted into the army, when his friends ran into him in the street and Mandelstam suggested to take a picture of the four of them with Liefshitz wearing a uniform. (SLM)

Listen to this good-old dandy,
Here's my theme:
All's a mish-mash, cherry brandy,
Cherubim.

There, where Helene's eyes are light with
Beauty's skin.
Through black holes I see the white with
Mortal sin.

Olive armies snatched That Helen
For the south,
As for me - just spume of heaven
In my mouth.

In my mouth, anointed by true
Poverty, —
Emptiness. A snook's been cocked to
Honor me.

Silly — really, head or tail,
All the same.
Angel Mary, down your cocktail,
Wine's the game!

Listen to this good-old dandy,
Here's my theme:
All's a mish-mash, cherry brandy,
Cherubim.

Translated by Eric Guth

Insomnia does speak: The Iliad. Tight sails.
The Ελλαξ ships stopped me amidst their half-read pages —
Some mournful wedding train of lonely brooding sages —
A soaring branch of cranes with beak to legs to beak.

Like sharpened arrow points — invading foreign lands,
Promoted Captain's heads with crests as pure as Heaven,
Why have you come so far? If She were not that Helen,
Would Troy be worth your time, O Achionic bands?

So Iliad, thus Sea — by love, both set in motion.
But which will speak to me? Yea hark, the book is closed.
As darkening-black sea comes crashing to the coast
I feel my head embraced by heavy, dreamless Ocean.
1915

Translated by Eric Guth

The front cover of Mandelstam's collection of poetry *Tristia*,
designed by Mstislav Dobuzhinsky. (SLM)

Alexander Mandelstam, Alexander Milman, Rurik Ivnev, Osip Mandelstam. Kharkov. 1919. (SLM)

Cherdyn in the Urals where Mandelstam was exiled the first time and where he tried to take his life. (A. Morozov's archives)

Just the books of my youth will I read -
Just the thoughts of my youth will I cherish, —
To be strewn far from woods, big and bearish;
Only then sorrow's pit can I seed.

I'm so mortally tired of this life,
So from life I'll accept nothing more,...
But my homeland — I love, though we're poor,...
For the earth, with poor homelands, is rife.

I once rocked in a faraway yard,
Up and down on a swing, coarse and wooden,
And dark limbs of tall pines still do brood on
A memory that grows hazy and hard.

Translated by Eric Guth

Poet Marina Tsvetayeva. 1916. In 1915-16,
Mandelstam was passionately in love with her. (SLM)

Olga Vaksel. 1920s.
Mandelstam's youth flame to whom he devoted many poems.
(Evgeny Mandelstam's archives)

Nadezhda Mandelstam, nee Khazina.
Osip met her in Kiev in the spring of 1919.
(Yuri Freidin's collection)

Nadezhda Mandelstam. 1920s. (Yuri Freidin's collection)

Delicate tenderness
The face I see,
A pale whiteness -
The arm you give me,
From universe whole
You stand off afar,
And all that you are
Cannot be avoided.

Cannot be avoided
The sorrow you feel,
From finger to heel
You're warm to the touch,
And the warning sounds
Of your despondent speeches,
Your distant reaches,
Know limitless bounds.

Translated by Eric Guth

And Mozart in bird's din, and Schubert near the water,
And Goethe whistling proud along a forest path,
And climbing frightful steps, the thoughtful Danish martyr
With fingers on crowd's wrist, believe in the crowd's breath.

Before a set of lips, perhaps was born the whisper,
As if in treelessness already twirled a leaf.
And those on whom this art's supposed to glister
Have features struck - pre-glister - with relief.

Translated by Eric Guth

A hollow, guarded noise is made
By fruit, self-plucked (without a warning),
Amidst the melody, unending,
of silent music - forest played.

Translated by Eric Guth

Osip Mandelstam. 1910s.
(Evgeny Mandelstam's archives)
A drawing by A. Zelmanova.

Alexander Mandelstam, Maria Petrovykh, Emily Mandelstam, Nadezhda Mandelstam, Anna Akhmatova. 1933, Moscow. (SLM)
The Mandelstams obtained a flat of their own (two rooms on the fifth floor, no lift, no gas stove, no bathroom) but they only managed to live there for six months before Mandelstam was arrested.

Osip Mandelstam. Voronezh, 1935.
The Voronezh exile turned out to be very fruitful for the poet. Here he wrote his "Voronezh Notebooks."

We live, deaf to the land beneath us,
Ten steps away no-one hears our speeches,
But where there's even half a conversation
Then the Kremlin mountain-man will be mentioned.

His black fingers are thick, grub-like,
And his words ring true, like lead weights,
His cockroach's whiskers laugh at us,
And the tops of his boots shine on us.

Around him a rabble of scrawny-necked leaders,
He plays with the fawning half-men
Who whistle, mew or whine,
Only he can direct and harangue.

One after the other his laws are forged, like horseshoes,
To be thrown in someone's groin, head, or eye,
Each execution is for him sweetness,
Our broad-chested Ossetian.

Translated by David Gillespie

С. С. С. Р.

1.

иненное Государственное Политическое Управление

ОРДЕР № 512

Мая 16 дня 1934 г.

дан сотруднику Оперативного Отдела ОГПУ

Герасимову

изводство Ареста - обыска

дельштам Осипа Эмильевича

есу Нащокинский пер. д. 5 кв. 16.

МЕЧАНИЕ. Все должностные лица и граждане обязаны оказывать

ому которого выписан ордер, полное содействие для успешного

Зам. Председателя ОГПУ

Начальник Оперативного Отдела

ка 309

On May 16, 1934, Mandelstam was arrested for "anti-Soviet verses", specifically his poem about Stalin. (KGB archives)

Osip Mandelstam, Nadezhda Mandelstam, Natalia Stempel, Maria Yartseva. Voronezh 1937. Natalia Stempel, then a young school teacher, preserved Mandelstam's unpublished verse for many years. (Yuri Freidin's collection)

Voronezh, the street where the Mandelstams lived. (V.Gordin's archives) Voronezh (Central Russia), his second exile town, where his wife joined him and they had a relatively good life there.

ЛИЧНОЕ ДЕЛО № 612

НА АРЕСТОВАННОГО

БУТЫРСКОЙ ТЮРЬМЫ ГУГБ НКВД

Мандельштам

Осип Эмильевич

прибыл 4/VIII 1938 года

Срок хран. ПОСТОЯННО

АРХИВ

опись

B13-2844

107794

Osip Mandelstam. On May 2, 1938, he was re-arrested. (KGB archives)
On August 4, 1938, Mandelstam was transported to the Butyrki Prison. The picture shows his prison file.

The poet and the prison... — unthinkable, monstrous combination, a criminal violation of the spirit of poetry, human rights and life itself.

Vladivostok today. The site of the former gulag, where in December 1938,

Mandelstam froze to death. His last letter reached his brother by a miracle:

"Dear Shura, I'm in the Vladivostok gulag, Barrack No.2. Got five years for counter-revolutionary activities. I was deported from the Butyrki prison in Moscow on September 9, and arrived here October 12. I'm in poor health, completely exhausted, emaciated, unrecognisable. I'm not sure there's any sense in sending me food, clothes or money.Perhaps you'll try sending me some warm cloths anyway. I'm freezing here..."

OSIP MANDELSTAM was one of the great poets of the 20th century, possessing as he did a prophetic understanding of its suffering and the gift to transform it into luminous poetry. Childish and wise, joyous and angry, at once complex and simple, he was sustained for 20 years by his wife and memoirist Nadezhda Mandelstam, who with Anna Akhmatova, became the saviour of his poetry.

Osip Mandelstam was born in 1891 and grew up in St Petersburg. Together with Akhmatova and Gumilyov he formed the Acmeist movement and in 1913 published his first book of poems, *Stone*. His second collection, *Tristia*, appeared in 1922, the year of his marriage to Nadezhda. 1928 saw the emergence of his third collection, *Poems*, and two prose works, the only other books he published during his lifetime.

In her memoirs *Hope Against Hope* and *Hope Abandoned* Nadezhda describes the Mandelstams' persecution under Stalin. After his arrest in 1934 she joined him in exile, first in the Urals and later in Voronezh. They returned to Moscow in 1937. On May 2, 1938 Mandelstam was re-arrested and sentenced to five years' hard labour for "counter-revolutionary activities". According to an official KGB letter received by Nadezhda Mandelstam, he died in December 1938 of "heart failure", in a freezing transit camp in eastern Siberia.

The Poet on Himself

I couldn't help but be affected by the October Revolution. It took away from me my "biography", my feeling of individual significance. I am thankful to it that, once and for all, it brought to an end any sense of spiritual security and the idea of living on cultural dividends... I feel indebted to the Revolution but I can only offer it gifts that it does not need for the time being.

I have no idea what kind of writer one should be. Answering this question would be tantamount to inventing a writer, and that is equivalent to writing his works for him.

Moreover, I am deeply convinced that for all a writer's dependence on and conditioning by the relationship of social forces, modern science does not yet possess the ability to create the desired type of writers.

Because of the embryonic state of eugenics, any kind of cultural grafting and cross-fertilization can give the most unexpected results. It would be easier to preserve the readers: for this end a direct method exits — school.

24 October 1928

Translated by Sonja Franeta

From "The Fourth Prose"

I love to come across my name in official papers, in judicial subpoenas and other austere documents. There my name has a most objective sound to it: a sound new to the ear and, it must be said, quite an interesting sound at that. I am often curious myself to find out what I have been doing wrong. Who is this Mandelstam chap, who for so many years has managed to dodge his duties, the villain?.. How much longer will he be able to get away with it? That's exactly why the years have passed me by without my reaping any reward. Others gain more respect with each passing year, but with me the opposite happens: time flows backwards.

I plead guilty. There can be no two ways about it, and there's no squirming out of my guilt. It's irredeemable. I've managed to dodge my duties. How much longer will I be able to keep it up?

When I am summoned by a tin-like subpoena, or a reminder comes from some public organization, Greek-like in its simplicity, when they demand that I betray my accomplices, cease my criminal activities, show them where I get my counterfeit money from, or sign a paper promising not to go outside the limits of a certain regulated area, I immediately agree. But then in the next breath I again begin to worm my way out. And so it goes on.

In the first place, I must have absconded once and they have to bring me back and lock me up, track me down and wash my brains. Secondly, it's a case of mistaken identity. I haven't the strength to prove who I am. I have my pockets full of useless trash: last year's coded notes, telephone numbers of relatives now dead, and addresses of people I don't know. Thirdly, I have signed with Beelzebub or the State Publishing House a grand but impracticable contract on Whatman paper (with a coating of mustard mixed with pepper and emery powder), which obliges me to return everything I have acquired illegally twice over, to belch back everything I have consumed illegally four times over, and to do sixteen times in succession the one and only thing that is impossible and unthinkable but that could in part bring about my acquittal.

With each passing year I get worse and worse. I feel like I've been drilled full of holes with a bus conductor's steel punch and franked with my own surname. I shudder every time someone calls me by my first name and patronymic — I just can't get used to it. What an honour! A Frenchman would be addressed as "cher maitre", dear teacher, but not me. "Mandelstam, comb the dogs' fur!" To each his own.

An aging man I comb the dogs' fur with the stump of my heart. But it's not enough for them, never enough... Russian writers look at me with canine tenderness in their eyes, imploring me to drop dead. Where does this time-servers' malice and boot-lickers' contempt toward my name come from? The gipsy at least had his horse, but I am gipsy and horse rolled into one...

Tin-like subpoenas are put under my pillow... the forty-sixth failed contract instead of a burial wreath, and a hundred thousand lighted cigarettes in place of candles...

No matter how hard I work, even if I carried horses on my back or turned millstones, I would never become one of the working masses. The work I do, no matter what expression it takes, is considered mischief, something outside the law, a mere irrelevance. Such is my fate, and I agree to it. I sign with both hands.

There are different ways of looking at things: for me, for example, the value of a doughnut is in its hole. What about the dough? A doughnut can be devoured up, but the hole remains.

Real work is like making fine lace — the important things are those that support the design, such as the air, the blunders, the absenteeism.

But for me, my feckless brethren, work reaps no profits, and isn't even entered on my record.

We have the Bible of Work, but we fail to appreciate it as such: Zoshchenko's short stories. The only writer who showed us the working man as he is, and we ground him into the dirt. I demand that monuments to Zoshchenko be put up in all towns and villages across the Soviet Union, or at least in the Summer Gardens, as was done for old man Krylov.

Translated by David Gillespie

Cold Summer

A team of four horses above the portico of the Bolshoi Theater... Thick Doric columns... Opera Square, an asphalt lake with straw-colored flashes from the trams — all are awakened at three in the morning by the clatter of unassuming city horses...

I recognize you, Bolshoi Theater Square — you are the umbilical cord connecting Moscow to the cities of Europe — and you are no better nor worse than your sisters.

And the Metropole, that dusty landmark, world-renowned hotel — under the glass roof I wandered around its street-like corridors

— occasionally coming upon a mirrored ambush or resting on wicker furniture in a quiet green. When I go out from the hotel and onto the square, temporarily blinded as I swallow the sunlight, my eyes are struck by the majestic reality of the Revolution. A great aria for a powerful voice drowns the buzz of automobile sirens.

Little ladies are selling perfume on Petrovka Street opposite the Mur-Merlise — pressed against the wall, an entire brood of them, tray to tray. This little row of vendors is like a small flock of sparrows, an army of Moscow girls with turned-up noses: sweet, hard working typists, flower girls, bare-legged — living on crumbs but blooming in the summer...

In rain showers they take off their little shoes and run through the yellow streams along the red clay of the soaking boulevards, pressing their valuable pumps to their breasts. They would perish without them: it's a cold summer. And like a bag of ice which cannot melt for anything, the cold hides away in some thick greenery in Neskuchny Park and from there creeps all over web-footed Moscow...

I recall Barbier's iambics: "When the oppressive heat burned through huge boulders." In the time when freedom was born — "this coarse tart the Bastille killer whale" — Paris went crazy from the heat. But we live in Moscow, grey-eyed and snub-nosed, in sparrow cold July...

I love to run out in the morning on brightly washed streets, through a yard, where during the night a summer snowdrift of puffy dandelions has appeared like a bed of feathers — and go right up to the kiosk to buy the latest issue of *Pravda.*

I love rattling an empty tin can like a little boy; going for kerosene not to the normal shops but to the slums. It's worth describing the place: an archway, then on the left a crude, almost monastic, staircase, two open stone terraces; hollow footsteps, the ceiling is oppressively low, stone slabs turned every which way; felt-lined doors; rope strung along like rigging; wily, haggard-looking children in long shirts throwing themselves under your feet; a real Italian yard. And in one of the windows behind a pile of trash you can always see a woman of indescribable beauty with a kind of face on which Gogol never spared his glorious metaphors.

He does not love cities who does not love its tatters, its modest, miserable little neighborhoods; who never gets short of breath on back staircases; who never trips over tin cans with the accompaniment of cats meowing; who never watches an airplane — a splinter in the azure sky — with its lively animal charm, from the prison-like yard at Vkhutemas...

He does not love cities who does not know its little habits: for example, when a horse-drawn carriage climbs up the hump of Kamergersky Street at a slow pace, beggars and flower-sellers would be following you...

At a big streetcar rest stop on the Arbat — beggars throw themselves at any streetcar to gather donations — but if the car is empty of riders, they do not move their spots and like beasts continue to warm themselves in the sun near the awnings of streetcar cleaning rooms. I saw how blind men played games with those who lead them.

And the flower-sellers move over to the side, spitting on their flowers.

In the evenings big games and revelry began on the thick green Tverskoy Boulevard — from Pushkin Square to the Timiryazev lot. How many unexpected things hide Moscow's green gates!

Passing by the eternally unchanging bottles on lottery tables, past three blind fellows singing "Talisman" in unison — toward a dark heap of people piled under a tree...

A person is sitting in the tree, one hand holding a long pole with a straw basket at the end of it and with the other hand, despondently shaking the tree trunk. Something is moving around the top of the tree. Yes, it's bees! Out of nowhere an entire hive together with its queen has flown in and settled on the tree. The obstinate hive hangs on the tree like a brown sponge and a strange beekeeper from Tverskoy Boulevard is shaking and shaking his tree over and over trying to get the bees to go into the basket.

It's so good to be in Streetcar A in a thunder storm, swinging through Moscow's green belt like a sash, chasing the stormy clouds. The city opens up at the Church of the Saviour in step-like chalky terraces, like chalky mountains they rise up from the city along with large river expanses. Here the heart of the city blows its bellows. And further out Moscow writes in chalk. The white dice of homes slips out more often. On the horizon of the leaden stormy sky, first we see the white towers of the Kremlin and finally the mad game of Solitaire in stone around the "Foundling Hospital," such a feast of stucco and windows like a honeycomb, an accumulation of sizes lacking majesty.

This Moscow deadly boredom alternates between enlightenment and inoculation — and when it begins to build, it cannot stop and rises like dough with every floor.

But I do not look for vestiges of the old life in this quaking, inflammable city: perhaps just a wedding party goes by in four carriages — the bridegroom, looking gloomy on his Name Day, the bride a white chrysalis; or perhaps in the middle of a pub, where with a beer they serve boiled peas with salted dry bread on a plate and a songleader marches out like a sturdy deacon and with a chorus of men begins to chime out God knows what liturgy.

Now it's summer — and precious fur coats are in storage in pawnshops: they are fire-red raccoon furs, fresh like they've just been bathed, and marten furs, all lined up next to each other on tables, looking like huge fish killed with harpoons...

I love banks — those menageries of moneychangers, where bookkeepers sit behind iron bars like dangerous animals...

It makes me happy when citizens have good shoes, when men wear gray English shirts, and when the chest of a Red Army soldier in uniform lights up like an X-ray, his crimson ribs.

1923

Translated by Sonja Franeta

Evgeny Mandelstam

Excerpts from Memoirs

I often used to smile at the idea of writing memoirs, thinking them an ailment that afflicted most old people. But the time came when I, too, succumbed. I shall soon be eighty, an age when for many of the elderly, events and persons, what one has lived through and seen, all these memories crowd the mind and demand expression. Even so, I might have resisted and not fallen a victim to this "ailment of the memoirs", had it not been for my duty towards by brother.

I feel an obligation to remember and record everything that I know about the short and tragic life of my eldest brother, the poet Osip Mandelstam. This is particularly important for an understanding of his early life. I am the only surviving member of the Mandelstam family, the only person who could write about the poet's family and youth, about his life before his marriage to Nadezhda Yakovlevna Khazina.

I shall start with the family's forebears.

Not a great deal is known about our mother's family, the Verblovskys. We can only say with any certainty that they belonged to the intelligentsia, with leanings towards European culture. Mother was closely related to the Vengerovs. Semyon Afanassievich Vengerov was an important literary historian and a Pushkin scholar: Isabella Afanassievna, his sister, was a professor of piano at the St Petersburg Conservatory. Other relatives on Mother's side included the extensive Kopelyansky family, who were wealthy business people. One of the sisters, the beautiful Lydia, married a Herr Kassirer, who lived in Berlin. Their son Ernest was a distinguished philosopher, a prominent representative of the Marburg School of Neo-Kantians.

My mother herself completed her schooling at the Russian Grammar School in Vilnius.

The ancestors of the Mandelstam family came from Zhagory, a town in the Shavel District of the Dvinsk Province in the Baltic. It was a gifted family, whose talented and energetic members succeeded in making their way in the world and moving on from Zhagory. The name of the physicist Academician Mandelstam, is well known. Old residents of Kiev still recall Professor Mandelstam, a famous ophthalmologist also active in social welfare. My brothers Maurice and Alexander Mandelstam occupied respected positions in the Leningrad medical circles. Another Mandelstam was a faculty head at Helsingfors University. Yet another was a dragoman and Arabic scholar, who worked in the Russian Embassy in Constantinople.

Zhagory was an insignificant little town. From time immemorial it had been a bastion of Orthodox conformism. The Jews, who accounted for a significant proportion of its population, were particularly devoted to national traditions and way of life. In our father's family the use of the Russian language and references to its culture, even for everyday communication, were forbidden. The Talmud and other sacred texts were carefully and respectfully preserved. All this was characteristic of life in the Jewish Pale.

Father's childhood and youth were difficult. Using his intelligence and enquiring mind, he strived to escape from the closed world of the Jewish community. Without his parents' knowledge, he would study by candlelight in his garret at night. He sought knowledge, and studied not Russian, but German. The urge to master German literature and philosophy characterized the whole of Father's life, reflecting to some extent the ties which have historically linked the Baltic States with Germany.

It was not long before Father found his homelife too oppressive and he escaped to Berlin. Here, far from his family, he could freely immerse himself in the works of Schiller and Goethe, of Herder and Spinoza. His straitened circumstances, indeed downright hunger, soon drove him to abandon his studies, and to return to the Baltic in search of a living wage.

My parents were married on the 19th January 1889 in Dinaburg (now Dvinsk). Father, Emile Venyaminovich Mandelstam, was then 33, and Mother, Flora Osipovna Verblovskaya, was 23.

Shortly after the wedding, Father learned the trades of glove maker and leather grader. The Dinaburg Handicraft Council gave him a testimonial on 27th February 1981, to the effect that "he was recognized as an acknowledged master". This imposing document, now yellowing after 85 years, issued "in the name of His Majesty the King", marks the beginning of Father's work in the leather trade.

The newly-weds soon found themselves in Warsaw. Here, according to the register of births and deaths, Osip was born, the darling and the pride of his parents. After the birth of their second son, Alexander, the family moved to St Petersburg, were they remained. There, in 1898 on Officers' Street, above Eiler's flower shop, I was born, the third and last child.

According to my mother, the main reason for moving to St Petersburg was the desire to give the children a good education, and expose them to the culture of which the city was a focus. As a Jew, Father could only obtain a residence permit by joining a merchant guild, which he proceeded to do. The diploma from the First Guild decorated the wall of Father's study.

This diploma, marking me as a merchant's son, almost caused me to lose my job in 1935, and it would have been difficult to find another after dismissal for such a reason. I turned for help to Korney Chukovsky, who as a friend of Osip's had been a frequent visitor at our home, and knew our family's circumstances. He wrote me a letter, saying that our family had always had difficulty making ends meet, that Osip never had any money and constantly borrowed money for his return trip from their house in Kuokkala or from Repin's house in Penates. In a postscript Chukovsky added: "I remember that some document, stating that your father was a merchant in some guild or other, used to hang in his study, but we all understood that this was simply protection against the Tsarist police."

Chukovsky was right. Our family's actual circumstances were far removed from the world conjured up by that diploma. Apart from a few years, when Father owned a small glove factory, he never had his own business, nor was he likely too. Father spent virtually his entire life dealing with leather as a raw material. He never had the means to buy skins and resell them to leather factories, but usually remained an intermediary between tanneries and leather processors.

Day by day, through the years and the decades. Father worked from dawn to dusk in cold sheds and warehouses, applying all his knowledge and experience to this difficult and physically demanding work.

He cherished the wish that one of his sons would follow him into the leather business, but we all chose other paths in life. Alexander and I sometimes helped Father with his business correspondence. I remember the pleasure it gave me to make copies on rice-paper using the massive, antediluvian press that stood in the corner of the study. Osip never shared in Father's work. Recalling in "The Noise of Time" — "the stale atmosphere of the trading room" (Father's study), he wrote with manifest distaste: "Even now it smells to me of slavery and hard labour, with the stench of tanned leather and the stretched kid-skins scattered across the floor, and chamois leathers lying there like living fingers..."

Nevertheless, in that same "stale" work-room there stood a book-case, that bore witness to both parents' craving for knowledge, for literature and philosophy, despite their differing predilections and tastes. Mother's and Father's books were placed separately. At the bottom, in the "Jewish Chaos", were the sacred texts, the Pentateuch, and a history of the Jewish People in Russian. Above stood German classics and philosophers. "With their help", as Osip expressed it, "Father forced his self-taught passage into the world of Germany out of the maze of the Talmud." Higher still stood Mother's books, Russian classics in early, or sometimes contemporary, editions. Osip, like his mother, loved old books and prized the external appearances. Many years afterwards, he asked me for Mother's Gogol in the Isakov edition of 1876, and also for her Pushkin as a keepsake in her memory.

Osip took the family book-case very seriously, as material evidence of relationships within his family. "The strata of the book-case showed all the tensions and stresses of the whole clan, and of the infusion into it of foreign blood". It was also his first repository of books which would go to form the grown man. "The bookshelves of early childhood accompany you for a lifetime. The selection of those books, the colour of their spines, will embody the colour, the quality, the disposition of world literature itself".

Our family was not an easy one. Its internal contradictions could not fail to be reflected in its behaviour. Father took no active part in family life. He was often gloomy, buried within himself. He scarcely bothered with us children, whereas we were the main reason for Mother's existence. He devoted all his time and effort to work. With age, and no doubt as a result of his abnormal working hours and mealtimes, Father often fell ill, suffering from migraines and stomach pains. Arriving home, he would shut himself up in his study and lie there the entire evening. We spoke in undertones in the house, and laughter and music were heard there less and less.

According to Osip, however, Father was much more gregarious in his younger years. He used to talk about his youth, his parents and his brothers. By the time I was about seven or eight, there was hardly ever an opportunity to sit down and talk with Father. Sadly, I cannot remember him once taking us for a walk or to the theatre.

With the passing of time, all the acute conflicts between Father and Mother left their mark and reappeared in different guises in each of the three brothers. Our domestic troubles had a particularly strong effect on Osip. This was understandable considering the sensitivity and susceptibility of his temperament. The older brothers scarcely ever asked their friends round to the house; their whole life was essentially spent outside the family circle, and remained unknown to the rest of us.

Osip's and Alexander's estrangement from the family became more pronounced as they grew older, and this aggravated Mother's sense of loneliness. She unwillingly sought comfort in me. By my eighth or ninth year, perhaps not so young after all, I was helping her with her household chores, and became her confident and counsellor. Perhaps because of my extreme closeness to my mother, I, despite everything loved our home. In any case I remember Mother with great tenderness and gratitude. She gave herself wholeheartedly to her children, and died so very young, at the age of just 48.

Mother lived alone. She had few friends. Among them was one good and honorable man, Yuli Rosenthal. He was an old bachelor, a banker and very involved in building one of the highways in the south-west. In the difficult periods at home — parental quarrels, complications over the children's education and so on — Yuli Rosenthal would always come round to the house. He was the "friendly spirit", as Osip called him, of our family, the guardian of our hearth. He could always restore peace, suggest what could disperse or alleviate problems with our relationships, make Mother feel better.

Rosenthal's visits were a joy not only for Mother. "A turbulent joy took possession of us children", wrote Osip, "every time Rosenthal's ministerial visage showed up — he bore a droll resemblance to Bismarck". We all discovered in him goodness of heart, wise counsel, and a solicitous attention to our welfare. He gave me my first wristwatch, which remained with me until 1942.

Late in his life, Rosenthal's generous heart and willingness to help was his downfall. He fell into the hands of a merchant family, the Oreshnikovs, who reduced him to poverty and sent him off to live out his last days, alone and half-blind, in a wretched room in Lesnoy Lane.

Osip and I felt profound compassion for Rosenthal, and we used to go and visit this dear old man. Dirty, neglected, cast aside, with a large magnifying glass in his hand and cataracts on both eyes, he daily read Suvorin's newspaper, the "New Times", from cover to cover.

The second person to visit us at home was Aunt Vera — Vera Sergeyevna Pergament, a relation of Mother's. She was exceptionally gifted, working for many years as secretary to senator M. M. Kovalevsky, who was an outstanding Russian economist and statesman. She translated Oscar Wilde and was an excellent pianist — Mother's usually silent grand piano would come alive under her skilful fingers.

In her youth Mother, too, had been a good pianist. She tried to instil and cultivate in us children a love and understanding of music. I took violin lessons as a child, and continued to play long into my adult life. Osip displayed an interest in music from an early age. As he remembered it, his "veneration" for symphony music started when he heard an orchestra at the Riga seaside when we were there as children.

For many years Osip had a passion for Wagner. This found an echo in his poetry. "The Valkyries and violins sing in unison: the unwieldy opera draws to its close: on the marble staircases stand the footmen, holding their masters' fur coats" Scriabin too was important to Osip. At that time he was conquering the hearts of musical St Petersburg, especially of the young people. In the old concert hall (now the Maly Philharmonic Hall), where once Liszt and Tchaikovsky played, Osip listened to many concerts conducted by Zilotti and Kussevitsky.

My brother also appreciated chamber music. His favourites were such fine singers as Butomo-Nazvanova, Zoya Lodi, Artemyeva. Later on he came to love the recitals of the pianists Chernetskaya-Geshelin and Maria Yudina. With the latter Osip and his wife established a friendship which endured until the last years of his life.

I do not need to say how important the Pavlovsk concerts were to the people of St Petersburg. Here at the Kursaal, Strauss conducted for several seasons, and there were performances by the greatest Russian and European virtuosi. In "The Noise of Time" Osip devoted a special chapter, "Music in Pavlovsk", to the atmosphere of Pavlovsk in the 1890s.

Mother always took one of us children along to the concerts at the Club of the Nobility. She did not miss a single performance by visiting musicians. She introduced us to the great pianist Hoffmann, the violinists Kubelik, Jascha Heifitz, and the 8-year old prodigy conductor Willi Ferrero.

Of Hoffmann and Kubelik, Osip wrote: "I never heard a sound of such primal clarity and sobriety, from the piano, like spring water, reducing the violin to the simplest indivisible voice made up of all its component filaments. I never heard such virtuoso Alpine cold, as in the spare, sober, formal clarity of those two masters of the piano and the violin."

Mother retained until the end her love of music, not only of the concerts but of the performers as well. Visiting performers at that time used to stay at the European Hotel, opposite the Philharmonic Hall, and often after concerts Mother, with us youngsters in tow, would take her place in the ranks of fans that formed out in the street. Sometimes, she even made her way into the hotel, and obtained a much-sought-after autograph. This happened when Hoffmann visited St Petersburg.

Mother also used to take us to the Mariinski Theatre. Every visit to the opera or the ballet was, for us children, a festival, transporting us into the world of dreams and fairy-tale images, the world of musical harmony, I remember not only our beloved operas, "Carmen", "The Queen of Spades". "The Legend of the City of Kitezh", and Wagner's "Niebelungen Ring", but also the constellation of brilliant performers who were the glory of Russian opera. I still recall the brilliant performances of Chaliapin, and Lipkovskaya, Yershov, Tartakov, Davidova-Delmas, who captivated Blok and inspired him to write his amazing verse cycle on the theme of Carmen, I remember the queues for tickets to hear Chaliapin. To obtain a seat, even in the gods, young people used to stand in line all night, warming themselves at campfires. It was a place for the nobility, the townsfolk and the coachmen to exchange their daily gossip.

Near the Mariinsky Theatre stood the Choral Synagogue. Each of us was taken there twice. Like for the concerts, we pressed for the Synagogue with great care. The best opera-singers were invited as cantors to the Synagogue.

However, visits to the Synagogue inspired no great pleasure in either myself or Osip, who returned as he put it, "heavily intoxicated". The synagogue, full of bearded old men with their prayer-shawls hanging over their shoulders, their muttering and swinging to and fro, produced an unpleasant, even distressing, sensation on my childhood spirit. This was exacerbated by the fact that the women sat apart from the choir, and I felt this was an insult to my mother.

Our constant moves from one apartment to another were an important part of our family life. In the long-ago years of my St Petersburg childhood, it was easy to rent an apartment that met any tenant's requirements, and it was rare to find a building that did not advertise one for rent. Mother was always extremely painstaking in her selection of a home, usually renting a 5- or 6-room apartment. My elder brothers usually shared a room, while I had a separate nursery bedroom. Grandmother also had a separate room, while the other rooms served as the dining room, the study, where Father effectively led his own life, and Mother's bedroom.

But however good the apartment. Mother was never satisfied. She was prey to a passion for moving house. The reasons were of the most unlikely kind, but usually they began to appear towards spring, after the habitual move of the previous autumn. Either she did not like the floor, or it was too far from the children's school on Mokhovaya Street, or else the rooms received too little sunlight, or perhaps the kitchen was inconvenient. By my reckoning, by the time of the 1917 February Revolution, we had moved seventeen times in St Petersburg. I can remember most of the apartments, even down to their floor-plans.

These frequent moves caused an inevitable disturbance in the rhythm of our family life. After the children and grandmother had been packed off to the dacha, all our furniture and belongings were put into store for the summer at the Kokorevski Warehouse. From the removal company came large covered wagons, drawn by heavy cart-horses. Stalwart removal men appeared with packing-cases, wood shavings and other packing materials, and took everything in hand. I remember they wore soft round leather pads on their heads, on which they carried the heavy items. Mother just gave the orders and directed what went into which packing-case.

Then began the crucial period of searching for a new apartment, the choice of wallpaper, and any necessary repairs. Later came the helter-skelter rush to have the apartment ready for the 1st September, the beginning of the new school term. Then the whole process was repeated in reverse order — from warehouse to wagons to the unpacking and making ourselves at home again in the new apartment.

Mother seemed constantly to be taking us to the dacha, and sometimes came to see us there herself. Both my brothers, Shura and Osip, loved these journeys, and went to the dacha not only in summer but in winter too, even when they were young men of 17 or 18. Several of these locations, where we used to rent our dachas, became treasured places for relaxation for Osip throughout his life, Pavlovsk and Tsarskoye Selo among them.

I have kept many childhood pictures, taken by local photographers. Osip repeatedly returned to these places in later life. Once he rented a room in the Chinese Village at Tsarskoye Selo, where the Karamzin house once stood. In the Twenties he and his wife Nadezhda rented a room in the lycee at Tsarskoye Selo. In our conversations together, Osip often used to recall that this had been one of the happiest periods of his life.

Father moved in with him when he was staying at Tsarskoye Selo. This was the one short period when father and son fulfilled their dream of living together. Osip's difficult financial circumstances, poverty plus his nomadic existence, all conspired to thwart this dream, and Father lived with my family until the end of his life.

Now, when I recall that distant past, I feel it is very important, in order to understand Osip's character, to mention that his relationship with his father underwent a profound change as he grew to manhood. His estrangement and complete lack of interest in his father's spiritual word was replaced by a deep and growing desire to grow closer to him. Father, in his final years, wrote something along the lines of a philosophical treatise. He wrote it in an almost illegible hand, and in German. Osip showed a great interest in this work, and took it away with him to decipher, and later on to discuss with Father. Unfortunately, after my brother's arrest, this manuscript disappeared. It is irreplaceable.

The Baltic roots of the Mandelstams, and the general popularity of the Riga seaside, were obvious reasons why, during our school years, Mother frequently took us children to Riga and to the "Strand" at Marienhof (Majori), as well as other places along that coast. In Riga we met Father's relations. His brother Hermann was in business there. Our Mandelstam grandparents were by then very old indeed. In their house reigned the same profound Orthodoxy that had been a characteristic of Father's family during his youth. This world was foreign to Mother, and we, so far as I can remember, restricted ourselves to infrequent visits to the old Mandelstams, only giving them what courtesy demanded. The joylessness of these meetings left their impression on my childhood spirit, and was confirmed in Osip's notes in "The Noise of Time".

The seaside, with its unending sandy beaches and dunes overgrown with pines, attracted us greatly. The kursaals and cafes, the evening music in the parks, the low prices and ease of accommodation drew a mass of holiday-makers. The beach was a picture, with its thousands of sunbathing bodies of all ages.

There was just one disadvantage: the sea along this coast was very shallow. Smart entrepreneurs offered, for a small price, bathing tents on wheels with awnings over their tiny balconies, and with steps down, which could be taken out into the water. These tents were of all colours: blue, green, red. A horse was harnessed to the tent and its rider drove us out to a deep spot, unhitched the horse, and returned to shore. In this manner whole families on their unusual "islands" would sunbathe, picnic, and swim all day. When the time came to return home, they would summon the driver, with a shout or a wave, and the horse would come to pull the tent back to shore.

When we went to Vyborg, we usually stayed with the Kushakovs. They were descendants of soldiers under Nicholas I. They had enjoyed certain privileges and settled in Finland where they grew rich from dealing in hides. They were clients of Father's and close family friends. The Kushakovs lived in a sturdy wooden mansion, beside which stood a stone building several stories high with a big shop at ground level. In the courtyard of this building was a sweet factory, where I was a constant visitor. The Kushakov family and their house retained to some extent the hearty, patriarchal atmosphere of a Jewish clan. Osip loved to come here. He was 17 or 18 then, and the Kushakovs had two delightful daughters with whom he was much taken. He courted one of them quite seriously, but the perfidious girl unexpectedly married an army bandleader, whose band played behind the stage during some of the shows at the Mariinski Theatre on occasions when they needed brass instruments. The marriage took place in St Petersburg. Kushakov Senior did not stint himself — he hired a special train of one pullman carriage. We were all invited to this family celebration, and transported in luxury to St Petersburg for the wedding. After the Revolution and Finland's independence we lost touch with the Kushakovs and I do not know what became of them afterwards.

From Vyborg our family would travel along the Saiminsky Canal to Vilmanstrandj, and from there to the Imatra Falls, the biggest in Russia. Imatra had a bad reputation — potential suicide cases used to go there from St Petersburg and throw themselves into the falls.

For several years running we rented a dacha on the shore of Lake Kuterselky. There our time was filled with boating, fishing, hunting for mushrooms and berries, and games with children from neighbouring dachas. The summer passed faster than we would have wished. My older brothers, naturally, consorted with boys of their own age. Osip always loved new places, taking a delight is nature, but at heart he always remained a town-dweller.

On the road outside our dachas, every day we would hear the cry of "Ice-Cream — plain or strawberry!", and round would come a two-wheel cart with its brightly-coloured box, and behind it the ice-cream seller in his white apron with a long spoon in his hand. He scooped the ice-cream from big metal containers and handed out the gaily-coloured cones. Osip has some wonderful, humorous lines about these small childhood pleasures: "Ice-cream: Sunshine! Puffy sponge-cake!..."

Osip loved Finland and travelled over a great part of it. He stayed with Korney Chukovsky at Kuokkala, with Repin at his house "Penates", or alone at guest-houses. He often took cures at the sanatorium at Hiuving, near Helsinki.

At that time there were many guest-houses, from the grand and stuffy to the small and democratic. Maxim Gorky's dacha stood beside the great Vamel-Jarvi Lake. There was a small house nearby, where the Linde sisters lived. They were music teachers and kept a small guest-house. Bed and board there were very cheap. Only friends came there, or people with an introduction, mainly students and school-children. The owners' brother, Fyodor Linde, was a Bolshevik, and among the lodgers of the guest-house there were quite a few young people of a revolutionary persuasion. In July 1917, Fyodor Linde led out on to the street the First Machine-Gun Regiment, quartered in Vyborg, and was shot by cadets, who were trying to return the troops to barracks.

Near the same holiday resort, on the edge of the forest in Mustameki, the St Petersburg doctor Rabinovich built a two-storey guest-house, very comfortable for those times, and it quickly gained a fine reputation. The owner was a long-standing friend of Mother's. His son, who was rather a bad lot, became friends with my brother Alexander. They were both courting the same girl, and there is a photo of the three of them in the guest-house garden. This guest-house became a magnet for the young Mandelstams in winter, and occasionally in summer also.

We used to play charades while on holiday. I remember once Osip and I thought up and played a charade on the name "Mandelstam". The first part was a sweetcake made from almonds, in the second was a treetrunk, and the whole was the two Mandelstam brothers, hand in hand. We often had musical evenings at the guest-house, playing new compositions, and reading poetry, though Osip always refused to read his own work.

At Christmas and on New Year's Day we used to go on sledges into the forest, where deep inside we would decorate a fir-tree, light candles on it, and build camp-fires. Osip took enormous pleasure in these diversions. He joked and laughed, delighting in his youth, still free from any shadow.

When it became time for the children to start school, Mother gave serious thought to where we should study. The state grammar and technical schools were in decline at that time, and our parents were attracted by the idea of private schools. There were a few such schools in the town: the Vyborg Commercial College (then the only co-educational school in Russia), the Tenishev College, and several others.

They tended to appoint more experienced teachers in such schools. There was a broad curriculum, and the best textbooks. But most important was the atmosphere, the whole soul of the school, which helped the school-child to find himself and develop his own character. Not everything about them was ideal, of course, but by comparison with the grammars, subject to the State, to the Ministry of Education which was notorious for its reactionary policy, the children here grew up in much better surroundings.

Despite the high cost, Mother's choice fell on the Tenishev College. Osip went there from 1898 until 1907. Alexander was also enrolled there, but did not work hard, and, at about the fifth class level, our parents transferred him to the First Grammar School. I entered the Tenishev College in 1907 and finished my schooling in 1916.

The College owed its name to its founder, the famous art-patron Prince Tenishev. Its headmaster, Alexander Yakovlevich Ostrogorsky was the noted teacher, social welfare enthusiast, and editor of the journal "Education". My brother always believed that the whole school rested on Ostrogorsky's smile. I can see him now, with his blond beard, prince-nez, and his wide smile. Just as he was in his photograph which every single pupil bought when he died.

At first the College was situated on Zagorodny Prospekt, and Osip began his studies there. Later on, a new building was especially erected at No. 33 Mokhovaya Street. Here the College was split between two buildings, connected by a gallery in which there was a conservatory and a fish-pool. How many wonderful moments and secret conversations must that conservatory remember!

The classrooms were light and spacious, the corridors broad. The chemistry and physics laboratories and the workshops were full of equipment. Instruction was heavily oriented towards practical work carried out by the pupils themselves. There was a gym beside the College, and during the forty-minute break there was always a game of football in progress, a game that was only just making its appearance in our country. Great attention was paid to our physical development, with a school doctor appointed to oversee this aspect. We first-formers had a dining-room by the College, where we received a hot breakfast and there were jugs of milk on the tables. All this, when we were young, was an unheard-of innovation. The abundance of food prompted ridiculous duels of gluttony to see who could eat the most cutlets or drink the most milk.

The buildings were immediately adjacent to a theatre and a lecture concert hall which gave directly on to the street. The theatre was not large, seating only about 300. During my schooldays, the Moscow Art Theatre gave guest performances there. I can still remember being deeply moved by the tragedy "The Death of Hope".

The concert hall, built in the form of an amphitheatre, with a double row of windows, was built for 800 people and intended originally to house the State Duma, but the government requisitioned the Tauride Palace for that purpose. The Tenishev Hall became a venue for concerts, and for social gatherings of considerable moment. Osip wrote that in this hall "...when something particularly important was taking place, people came to blows and the whole Mokhovaya Street was boiling over with floods of policemen and intellectuals."

In the 1900s, when Osip was attending the College, the hall was very often hired by the Literary Foundation, which staged memorial evenings in honour of various writers.

Meetings of the Lawyers' Society took place in this same hall, headed by Maxim Kovalevsky and Petrunkevich. Many orators spoke here, carrying out, in Osip's words, their "civic duties", reading their lectures. Although Osip used to describe the evenings of the Literary Foundation with unconcealed and sometimes even malicious irony, still it cannot be disputed that the close proximity of the hall to the College played a favourable part in the upbringing of the Tenishev pupils. It was helping to instil into them a love of literature and a sense of civic responsibility by introducing them to contemporary problems, albeit from a liberal-bourgeois standpoint.

In my time and afterwards, the Tenishev Concert Hall became even more closely connected with the cultural life of St Petersburg.

It became a favourite locale for writers and poets to read their work, and for literary discussions. Here we listened to the young Mayakovsky, who used to wear a yellow shirt on stage. Osip too read his poetry here frequently. I myself put on an evening of "contemporary poetry and music" in this hall for the benefit of wounded soldiers, in which many writers and poets, including my brother, took part.

The Tenishev College had a system of semesters — instead of eight school years, it had sixteen semesters. The pupils advanced from semester to semester, twice each year. The preparatory class was also divided into two semesters, the preparatory itself and the intermediary. Before passing from one semester to the next, a report was always drawn up by the teachers, covering all subjects, and this was shown to the parents.

Every effort was made to encourage study of the humanities, and to improve the pupils' writing style. Class and college periodicals were also encouraged. When our schoolmate Feinberg died, the pupils got together and published a small collection of his verse. Our class, over a period of years, published a lithographed journal "Young Thought". I edited it, published some of my short stories, and often acted as its theatre critic into the bargain.

In almost all subjects, the teachers at the Tenishev College were superior in knowledge and talent to the ordinary grammar school teachers of those days.

Outstanding was the literature master, Vladimir Vassilievich Gippius, a well-known expert on Pushkin. He was the cousin of the poetess Zinaida Gippius, the wife of Merezhkovsky. His brother Vassily Vassilievich Gippius was also a poet.

Vladimir Gippius had his own teaching methods. He recognized no textbooks. He read out his lectures, enthralling his class with a brilliant exposition of the most interesting material. At each lesson a pupil was appointed to take detailed notes, and at the next class, before embarking on a new topic, these notes were revised and discussed. At the end of the school year, all these notes were copied and formed the basis for revision and the examinations. Naturally Gippius's lessons were the best-liked.

Chemistry was taught by Vadim Nikandrovich Verkhovsky, a good man with a pleasant personality and the author of the best textbook of those days, which was still in use many years later in Soviet schools. Albert Petrovich Pinkevich taught natural history, in a lively and attractive fashion. He and the mathematics teacher G. M. Fichtengolz later rose to a professorship.

Much of the experience of the Tenishev College went into the later development of comprehensive schooling, since Pinkevich became a close collaborator of Lunacharsky at the State Committee for Education, and he played an important role in the reforms of high-school education after the October Revolution.

Apart from lessons, excursions also figured prominently in the educational programme at the Tenishev College. These took place at the end of each school year. The founders of the school and its teachers deserve gratitude for them! The College had a strictly organized system of increasingly complex excursions, beginning with one to the Udelninsky Park for walks, butterfly-catching, and plant studies. In succeeding years there were longer visits to Moscow, to the Dnieper, to Kiev, and before finally finishing school, the biggest excursion of them all, to the Urals. Long before the end of the school year the coming excursion became the main subject of conversation, the relevant books were read, and all the plans drawn up.

The trip to the Dnieper impressed me mightily. I don't remember all the places Osip went to, but I still have a postcard from him to our parents as evidence of his Novgorod trip.

It is impossible to overstate the wonderful atmosphere of unity and friendship that reigned at the Tenishev College. No uniform was worn by either pupils or masters, unless you count the unwritten tradition with an unknown origin, that pupils should wear Russian high boots. School uniform, as a form of discipline, was quite foreign to Tenishev schoolboys. The whole atmosphere and the absence of formality themselves maintained discipline among pupils.

Everything co-existed, everything interacted in the melting-pot of the school. Democracy was there, despite the exceptionally varied social status of the schoolboys. Here the sons of the general staff, of bankers, of shop-owners, of architects, doctors, barristers, and other members of the professional classes, got on together, and there was no arrogance shown by one towards another. Those who had carriages and automobiles left them far from the school gates, and the boys entered the college on foot, making no show of their parents' wealth or position in society.

Both Osip and I loved our school. I was ready to liken it to the Pushkin Lycee, and if, in the course of a long life, I happened to meet or hear of a classmate, it warmed my heart, and there was always something to remember, to talk about. True, nowadays hardly any are left — many have died, and some emigrated after the October Revolution.

Osip's warm attachment to our school was illustrated by a tragic episode, recounted to me by Evgeny Kreps. In those desperate days of 1938, before his death in the camp near Vladivostok, Osip was in the infirmary, where he was dying of physical and psychological dystrophy. His mind was clouded. It just so happened that the head doctor at the infirmary was an old Tenishev boy, Evgeny Kreps, at that time a prisoner, but later an academician and a famous physiologist. Kreps never liked to recall what he had been through, but he did once tell me that, knowing about Osip's illness, and that he was in this particular camp, he went to his bedside and said: "Osip Emilievich, I am a Tenishev boy too! That appeared to be sufficient to restore my brother to consciousness for some minutes, and they spoke of their youth. According to Kreps, Osip mentioned me.

Let us now look a little more closely at the details of Osip's time at school. At the preparatory class. Osip and the other children became the charge of that silver-bearded miracle-maker Nikolay Platonovich Vukotich, who hailed from Serbia, a man who dedicated his entire life to budding children. He took Osip's preparatory class, as he was later to take my own.

We can form an opinion of Osip in the junior classes not just from his and my recollections. I have kept a curious document — "Report of the Achievements and Behaviour of Osip Mandelstam Third-Form Pupil of Tenishev College for the Year 1901/1902." It is a list of his various subjects. Even in the third form, several teachers noted character traits that Osip was to display all his life. Perhaps the most interesting observation was that of his geography master. "A very clever and unusually industrious boy, upright, very impressionable and sensitive to dislike or reproof, speaks well..."

Osip's interests defined themselves early on. From childhood, he had a vocation for the humanities and for theoretical work, while the exact sciences and practical work drove him to irritation and lethargy. He liked geography, history, natural history (see his verses about Lamarck), and languages. Literature, of course, was the most important to him. His studies quickly took him beyond the boundaries of the curriculum. This was already evident in his third-form report. In essence this was a testimonial not to his mastery of the school curriculum, but to his formation as an individual. His teacher wrote: "He has made great strides in the past year. Exceptional progress can be observed in his independence of thought and ability to express himself on paper."

I cannot quite recollect which master wrote this report — it was either Gippius or Osip's first literature teacher. It does not matter. Osip was certainly a pupil of Gippius, and belonged to those who kept up an inner bond with the teacher. In 1923 Osip wrote: "The power of Vassily Vassilievich's appreciation still holds away over me".

Osip had the greatest respect for Gippius as a teacher. Firmly convinced of his outstanding talent and personality, Osip called Vassily Vassilievich "a moulder of the spirit and a teacher of outstanding men" and adds in parentheses "only, these were few and far between". Time has proved the accuracy of Osip's observation — among Gippius's pupils Osip himself and Vladimir Nabokov were outstanding both as writers and as individuals.

But let us return to our third-form Mandelstam. It is interesting that in his report all the teachers mention Osip's application, regardless of subject. It does not matter whether it is his favourite subject, natural history ("very interested in the subject, worked diligently and mastered the course work well"), geography ("he loves the subject and works twice as hard as necessary"), or German ("has a marvellous affinity for the subject"). His endeavour does not flag even with those subjects which he regards as a penance. Thus Osip "tries to accomplish something in handicraft, even though he considers the subject a real torment as do the majority of children who suffer from a nervous disposition and poor health." And he goes on "... we suffocated amid sawdust and woodshavings, unable to saw a plank of wood in half. The saw stuck, the plane bent, we hit our fingers with the chisel, nothing came out right..."

Osip's assiduity, however, soon began to wane. The distractions that awoke with each passing year interfered with his studies. Alexander, my second brother, became so interested in chess and the races that in the fifth form he had to be taken away from the Tenishev College, where the academic requirements were above average, and transferred to a grammar school. Things were little better for Osip, despite his outstanding talents. Mother had to have recourse to home tutors. For us Jewish children the need for a gold medal on leaving school hung over us like the sword of Damocles. It was the key to our entry into higher education: Jews were not allowed to make up more than 5% of the student population. Our tutors were "perpetual students" with some revolutionary connections. Describing one of them Osip pointed out that he was not yet a true revolutionary, just a "tutor in revolution". "He spouted revolutionary phrases, which rustled in my head like cigarette paper in the cold." But for all that Osip emphasized that there was something "of the gendarme" about him. In the crucial days of 1905, he took no part in the revolution.

Our coaching under our tutors, in whose company, as Osip said, "the wind of revolution" burst into our home, coincided with the high-water mark of the revolution, its retreat, and the reimposition of reactionary power. Osip lived through the 1905 Revolution much the same as most young people, hoping for and expecting great things. His sympathy for these revolutionary events was enhanced by his proximity to the Sinani family, who exerted considerable influence over him. The head of that family was a well-known doctor, and his son Boris was a classmate and close friend of Osip's. They were fanatical Socialist Revolutionaries. There were constant arguments at their home, discussions about the differences of opinion between the Social Revolutionaries and the Social Democrats, the platform of the Populist Party, the role of individual leaders in history, etc.

Despite his knowledge of the differing currents of socialist thought, his interest in the ideas of his time, Osip did not become a partisan of any one party. He was drawn into the complex tangle of all these conflicting ideas and drank deeply at the well of all the attitudes prevailing during those years.

Side by side with his serious interests, both ideological and literary, Osip liked to be side-tracked by diversions. He was something of a dandy in his youth. He had a weakness for fine shirts and ties, and liked to send his linen to the Chinese laundry. He enjoyed riding in smart cabs. He needed money for concert and theatre tickets, but Mother could not always manage to give him enough pocket money. On such occasions Osip tried to raise the necessary funds some other way. I can remember how, in the morning over breakfast, our maid Anyuta would say to Mother: "Madam, the doorman is in the kitchen, waiting — Osip Emilievich came home late last night and borrowed fifty kopecks from him to pay off his cab." In those days the pawnbroker was a frequent helper over a difficult moment. Mother too used to use him when money was low. However, occasionally she found receipts for silver spoons pawned secretly by Osip. This caused her much distress.

The bookcase housing my childhood library was one source of ready money for my elder brothers. More than once I commented on the disappearance of my favourite books, sold by my elder brothers to the second-hand book-dealers. These were bitter moments. Unlike Osip, I was an enthusiastic craftsman. I had my little workshop in the house, and I even employed the fruits of my school studies in electricity. In order to save my treasures from the banditry of my brothers, I built a signalling system from my bookcase into the corridor, so that when it was opened, a buzzer sounded and a lamp lit up. But all this was of little avail.

On the slightest pretext, Mother always liked to indulge her children, especially Osip. By virtue of being the first-born, he was the favourite, and Mother's concern for him was understood and acknowledged by the entire family. My brother's awareness of his gifts began early, and, as the family atmosphere became more difficult, he began to exhibit a certain egocentricity, to assume that everyone around him should serve him. Thus, from this childhood indulgence, the threads extended into his later life. In the years of his fame and recognition as a poet, as in the disorderly years of his poverty, Osip retained his self-confidence and very often when in company would insist on his right to exclusivity, carrying this trait not only into his daily life but into his business dealings with printers, publishers and the Writers' Union. At such moments he could write or say very offensive, even abusive, things to people. He was explosive, flaring up very quickly but as quickly cooling off.

There were certain aspects of Osip's behaviour that on occasion set people against him and gave his enemies material for criticism, hostility or censure. But this had little substance for those who appreciated Osip's rich spiritual world — they prized his poetic gift and understood to what a Path of the Cross he had condemned himself in life and in literature. Nothing could prevent his friends and relatives from respecting and loving him, just as he was in life and remained in the memories of his contemporaries. In spite of his difficult temper, his great goodness should not be forgotten; his selflessness in his relationships with others was characteristic of him.

I was myself more than once the beneficiary of his kindness. Osip used to take me to the doctor, whenever there was a suspicion that I might be seriously ill. I often felt lonely and Osip used every opportunity to cheer me up. He came to see me at the time of both my first arrests. Once he travelled to see me at the place where we, the prisoners, were working. On the second occasion he came to the special prison train just before our departure for Moscow. I am indebted to his efforts for my release from my third term of imprisonment, when I was threatened with internal exile.

His letter to me of December 1923 radiates much warmth. It was written at a time of great hardship for me when, after my release from prison, I could neither regain my place at the university nor find another job. Although Osip could offer me no help, his letter remains very dear to me: "... I desperately want to help you. But I haven't a kopeck to spare. I've only got 40 roubles to last me the next two weeks. Things will get much better after the holidays. You know me. If only I could see you, I'd think only of you. That's the way I am. Come in two weeks, then I'll be with you all the time. It's terrible that we can't live together..."

My brother's good intentions were entirely sincere. He was the most kind and impulsive of men. I knew that when somebody close to him and needing his help was actually with him, then he would do anything for that person and forget utterly about himself.

All his life Osip showed love towards children. I remember this well, and saw it in his relations with my own children, especially in the case of my late daughter, killed in the Siege of Leningrad. I think that my brother's own childlessness not only deprived him of the joys of fatherhood, but perhaps was also in some way reflected in certain aspects of his spiritual make-up.

Osip's years in the senior classes of the Tenishev College were spent during the uneasy years of 1904/07. After the defeat of the first Russian revolution in 1905, St Petersburg was a troubled place. This was the time of the Black Hundreds, the Monarchists of the Saint Michael the Archangel Union, who preached the massacre of the Jews and the arrest of insurgent workers and students. The press wrote of infamous pogroms in the south of the country, of instances of outrageous antisemitism. I can remember Father keeping in his bedside table an elegant lady's revolver, to protect his family against any danger. That revolver was a symbol of the situation threatening the habitual order of things.

Mother was a prey to worry, to the fear of pogroms. She was afraid that even here in St Petersburg, with the silent blessing of the authorities... In search of safety, she sent us off to the suburbs, to Pavlovsk or to Tsarskoye Selo, where, so it seemed to her, there was no chance of such excesses.

In 1907, the year Osip finished school, Mother was afraid of something else: his friendship with young revolutionaries. Frightened that he might be arrested, Mother decided to send Osip to Paris, where she had friends. There is no evidence that Osip was in any real danger. He took no direct part in revolutionary activities. But Mother's caution did not seem exaggerated, and Osip's trip to France opened up a new world to him and contributed much to his development.

Osip lived on the outskirts of Paris in a small villa belonging to friends of the family. Paris opened before Osip unbounded opportunities to commune with beauty in painting and in culture. He went to lectures at the Sorbonne, he visited museums and architectural monuments. His love-affair with Paris later found ample expression in Osip's work.

After about a year my brother had to return to St Petersburg.

But neither he nor Mother abandoned the thought of his continuing his studies in one of the European centres of learning, and at the first opportunity Osip did indeed go abroad to resume his studies.

Mother's health required her to undergo treatment in a sanatorium, and as people did then, she would go abroad to a resort to "take the waters". She took me with her, and Osip often came to see us. I remember arriving early in the morning at Berlin's Friedrichbahnhof, and being amazed that the streets were not only washed down, but scrubbed with brushes. Our sanatorium was not far from Berlin, and Osip came to join us there.

He also joined us at Beatenburg, a small Swiss spa in the mountains, 1.200 metres above sea level. There we took walks together through the Alpine meadows, fell in love with the snow-capped peaks stretching away above the lake and the view of the tidy toytown of Interlaken below. These were good times, and Osip, with prospects just opening before him, was happy. He often recalled Beatenburg in later life.

I must make a small digression at this point. I have often been asked whether my brother ever went to Italy. I replied that to the best of my knowledge he had never been there. Then suddenly in my old age, when I was looking through my papers in Leningrad, I came across a postcard with a view of Italy, addressed to the dacha in Finland to our brother Alexander. "Shurenka! I'm off to Italy! It has happened just like that. I have only 20 francs — but never mind. One day in Genoa, a few hours by the sea, and back to Bern. I even like this mad rush. The train follows the narrow valley of the Rhone. It's a sheer wall — cliffs and forest curtained with clouds. They (Mother and I) don't know about it yet, of course." So, leaving Mother and me behind on some pretext or other, he did go to Italy and breathed its air, albeit only for a couple of days.

In the autumn Osip went to Heidelberg, where he studied under the professors of that illustrious university. We met him again in that ancient town, where Mother went to call on her son and see how he was getting on. Osip showed me around the town and the castle, now a museum. This was the first time I had found myself in such medieval surroundings. Being a child, I remembered of course the faces of the students — guildsmen with scars, the results of duels with students from other guilds, and the different-coloured hats, signifying the regions they came from.

Osip returned to St Petersburg in 1911. The family did not allow him to finish his course at Heidelberg, but it must be said that his studies there and at the Sorbonne contributed much and formed the basis of his broad education in philology. They also helped his poetry too. We must be grateful to Mother for managing to stretch the slender family budget enough to pay for her gifted first-born to have an education abroad.

Back in Russia, Osip decided to complete his education by applying to study in the history and philology faculty at the University of St Petersburg, which at that time, judging by the professorial staff, was one of the best in Russia. The faculty was headed by Zelinsky and a number of other eminent scholars.

To enter the university, however, there was first an obstacle to be overcome. Osip's school-leaving certificate was modest, and all the restrictions on the entry of Jews into higher education applied to him. We had to consider having him baptised as a Christian. That removed all the restrictions, because in Tsarist Russia the Jews were persecuted mainly because they belonged to another faith.

Mother had nothing against such a solution, but for Father Osip's baptism was a matter of extreme grief. The procedure to change one's faith was not complicated, involving only the exchange of documents and a small monetary fee.

A certain Pastor Rozen in Vyborg, who belonged to a rather small episcopalian methodist church, counting a worldwide community of about one and a half million people, helped Osip became a protestant. Osip had no idea, of course, how the episcopalian-methodist church differs from other religious denominations.

Mother became aware very early of her eldest son's literary talent. It was noticed too at the Tenishev College. Osip wrote no childhood verse, and when he did begin to write, at the age of about 16, he never read his poems at home, not even to Mother. In 1908 Osip sent a short letter with 16 youthful poems to Vyacheslav Ivanov, hoping to have them published. This poet was one of the pillars of Russian Symbolism, the master to whom everyone listened and against whom all poets measured themselves. Not one of Osip's poems was published and when in 1913 he was preparing his first collection, he himself, did not include any of them.

Later on my brother used to visit Vyacheslav Ivanov in his "tower", where on Wednesdays some interesting poets and prose-writers, critics, philosophers and musicians used to gather. There they read aloud new poems, discussed symbolism, the future of literature and new trends in poetry.

Osip's first poems were published in the journal **Apollo** in 1909, and at about this time also in another journal, **Education**, whose editor was the headmaster of the Tenishev College, Alexander Yakovlevich Ostrogorsky.

The story of the publication of *Stone*, a slim volume of 58 poems written between 1908 and 1913, is interesting. *Stone* was published at the author's expense, the money being put up by Father, in an edition of only 600 copies. I remember the day when Osip took me to the printers on Mokhovaya Street and we took delivery of the printed edition. The author took one parcel, and I took the other. We were faced with a problem — how to sell them. Bookshops in St Petersburg would not purchase verse collections, but only accepted them on a commission basis. They only made an exception of a very few well-known poets, such as Blok. After much deliberation, we gave the whole print-run on commission to the big bookshop of Popov-Yasni, on the corner of Nevsky Prospekt and the Fontanka.

Osip sent me from time to time to check how many copies had been sold, and when I told him that 42 had already gone, there was rejoicing at home. In the context of the book business at that time, this sounded like the first recognition of the poet. Whoever studies Osip Mandelstam's poetry is aware that in this first collection he already stands forth as a great poet, with a fully-developed poetic credo. He at once assumed a distinguished position among contemporary poets.

In 1914 the Great War began. It had its echoes even at school. They introduced military training at the Tenishev College, we were given old rifles, and issued with khaki tunics and trousers. There were drills in the school yard. I was most interested by the drums, whose beat accompanied our square-bashing. The drummer-boy was me!

On the whole the war excited me. It is interesting that the only poem I ever wrote in my life was dedicated to the Russo-Japanese War, I was only seven at the time. The poem was dreadful and utterly chauvinistic, describing how the Japanese ran like cockroaches before the valiant Russian warriors. And this was when the whole country was grieving over the Battle of Tsushima and the fall of Port Arthur. My older brothers and especially Osip happily poured scorn on my doggerel and teased me. I was terribly offended by this, flew into a rage, but they just laughed at me.

At the start of the First World War, I was already 16 and reacted differently from my brothers to the unfolding events. They remained more or less indifferent to the war, whereas I at once involved myself in aid to the wounded, which was very much the responsibility of the Russian intelligentsia. The Tsarist government, unequal to this task, had to permit the establishment of two powerful organizations — "The All-Russia Union of Municipalities" and the "Land Assembly", each of which possessed its own network of field and city hospitals and its own ambulance fleets. They were financed by social funds and private donations.

We Tenishev students managed to involve ourselves in help to the wounded. A Central Field Hospital Committee was formed and I became its representative. We collected money and the ten and fifteen kopeck coins mounted up into a sizeable sum. With this money we supported 20 beds in Hospital Number 11 of the Union of Municipalities. This hospital was housed in an old eighteenth century building which had been the herbarium of the Botanical Gardens.

Here individual donors and organizations could pay the costs of the beds.

I was often at the hospital. I took a course first as a medical orderly, then as a male nurse, and began voluntary work there. At about the same time I helped with the students' transport fleet, at the Warsaw Station, where the hospital trains arrived from the front. The wounded were taken by ambulance and specially-equipped trams to hospitals all over the city. We helped to unload these trains.

In the winter of 1916 with Osip's help, I organized an "Evening of Contemporary Poetry and Music" in the concert hall of the Tenishev College. The proceeds were to go to help the wounded. The performers were to be the most famous poets and musicians, and we were wholly successful in securing their services. I still have the programme of that concert, the expenditure accounts, the net receipts, which we transferred to our hospital, and even a cutting with a review from the newspaper *The Day.*

The performers included the young Sergey Prokofiev, who played his first piano sonata, the popular singers of the day Butom-Nazvanova and Artemyeva, who sang romances and arias. Poems were read by Blok, Akhmatova, Kuzmin, Mandelstam, Klyuev, Ivanov, Gumilev, to name a few.

I accompanied our patroness A. Avilova in her luxurious French automobile, making the rounds of all the performers to ask them to take part in this charity concert. Let me tell you about my visit to Yesenin. He was then a close friend of Nikolai Kluyev, a gifted "country" poet from Veliky Ustyug. They lived together somewhere by the Kryukov Canal. Klyuev met us at the door, dressed in an ordinary suit. He excused himself, saying he was not "properly dressed", and that he would change and return with Seryozha. A few minutes later he reappeared in a peasant coat and Russian high boots, with his hair pomaded. In a strong northern accent he said: "May I introduce you — this is Seryozha." This transformation, this mask of rural simplicity, looked altogether forced and unnatural on such an educated and well-read man, who was just finishing his studies in the philology faculty of St Petersburg University. I saw Yesenin as everyone remembers him from that time — a blue-eyed lad from Ryazan, curly-haired and smiling. Although he had only recently arrived in the capital, he was already famous. He was a great favourite, and his public readings always drew a full house.

Blok and his wife Lyubov gave us a friendly reception at their flat in Pryazhka. It was small and modestly furnished: his study was full of books and had a white-tiled stove. I, like the rest of my generation, idolized Blok, and he remained all my life a congenial, exciting and invigorating poet.

It was the evening of the concert. The auditorium was packed, with sold-out notices outside. The police were turning away those without tickets. Akhmatova read during the first half, to loud applause. Osip read "Phaedra" — "I shall not see Phaedra in this old, many-tiered theatre"... His chiselled verses read in that distinctive voice, a light singing monotone, did not reach everybody in the auditorium and, as the critic wrote, the St Petersburg public preferred Akhmatova's "Lyricism of the heart".

Blok was supposed to perform in the second half. I went to fetch him in Avilova's automobile. Lyubov Blok received me doubtfully, and said that "A. B. isn't going anywhere, he's in the bath, there's been some misunderstanding. Tears came into the eyes of this young organiser. Blok's wife calmed me down and, asking me whether the car was open or had the hood up, departed for a discussion. She returned from the bathroom with cheering news — Blok would come, but asked for a little time to cool off after his bath. Hoorah! I was riding with Blok in person, talking all the while with Blok himself! How simple he was in his personal relationships, how solicitously he asked about the hospital, about my doings at school. Anyone who saw into his eyes or listened to his light baritone voice, will never forget him. There is no need to speak of the success of his performance, the applause which greeted his appearance and accompanied his departure from the stage. I often heard Blok afterwards, but the evening of which I write was the first and it was unique for me.

At the end of 1916, Milyukov, Kerensky, Guchkov and Shingarev were rousing the public with their speeches in the State Duma, harshly and openly criticizing the decaying regime. The speeches were very successful, they were multiplied and spread. We printed in semi-secrecy on our duplicator at the hospital. We almost paid dearly for this. We were threatened with an inspection from the Prince of Oldenburg, but we learnt of it in time and were able to hide all the seditious publications, especially removing from the library all books unsuitable for "the soldiery". The inspection passed off well, and I was even presented with a medal "For Zeal". The February Revolution rescinded this award.

In the second half of the summer of 1915, Osip suggested to Mother that she should take us both to Koktebel in the Crimea to see Voloshin. Osip had met him in 1906 at the home of I. A. Vengerova, a relative of Mother's. Voloshin remembered Osip then as a boy "with dark squinty eyes, his haughty nose in the air."

We took the train to Feodosia and from there reached Koktebel, which was then only a small village, on horse-back. The poet, painter and philosopher Maximilian Alexandrovich Voloshin had built himself a house there as early as 1903, and in the 1910s and 1920s it became a place of relaxation and a meeting-point for writers, painters, scholars and musicians. Marina Tsvetaeva was quite right when she said of Voloshin that his true vocation was "to draw people together, to bring about destinies and meetings."

The architecture of Voloshin's dacha was distinctive. It had several extensions with small whitewashed rooms almost devoid of furniture for the use of visitors. Customs here were simple and undemanding. Only his friends, or people recommended by his friends, were invited. All gatherings were held in the tower-room, where the most fascinating discussions and conversations took place. It had an uninterrupted view over a chain of mountains and the sea. Arguments and poetry-readings continued here from early evening deep into the night.

I have kept a photo from 1915 of Voloshin in his tunic and of Julia Lvov in the tower-room. This guest of Voloshin was a friend of Osip's and the mother of Olga Vaxel (Lyutik), who played an important role in my brother's life.

Julia Lvov was attracted to theosophy and took an active part in the meetings of the Free Philosophical Society in St Petersburg. Osip was himself interested in theosophy. There were quite a few famous names in the ancient Lvov family. Lvov's grandfather, Lyutik's great-grandfather, was a world-famous violinist. He wrote the music for the hymn "God Save the Tsar". A Lvov was the first director of the Imperial Chapel Choir in St Petersburg.

I took my final examinations in May 1916 and so completed my secondary education. I was so sad to leave the Tenishev College, which had become a second home! The future was full of promise and yet frightening. I had to think about work, about higher education.

With my childhood liking for engineering I decided to apply for a place in the electro-mechnical faculty of the Peter the Great Polytechnical Institute, one of the best higher education institutions of its kind in the country, with splendid buildings, well-equipped laboratories, and eminent professors.

Imagining myself in the handsome uniform — dark-blue double-breasted jacket with epaulettes brilliantly embroidered with the monogram P-I, I dreamed of my successful entry. Could I jump the last hurdle? I was worried not by the high competition, but by the percentage restriction on Jewish entry. I had my gold medal, but there were several dozen gold medal holders among the Jewish applicants, and only six places open to them. In such circumstances, they had recourse to a lottery, and this still lay ahead.

I wanted to find some job for the summer, a plan of which Mother approved. I had already begun to earn money for my personal expenses during my last years at school, giving lessons to the young son of a rich family. My first wages meant my first gifts to my parents and the chance to manage my own finances — all this was most gratifying.

I succeeded in finding a job at the floating hospital of the Petrograd Committee of the Union of Municipalities. The seaship "Grand Duchess Xenia", which plied the Volga between Nizhny Novgorod and Astrakhan, was transformed into a floating hospital for convalescents, and was the first hospital of this kind in Russia.

While I was sailing the Volga, my brother again went to Koktebel. On the way, Osip stopped at Alexandrov and spent a week with Marina Tsvetayeva. She lived there in her dacha with her daughters and their nanny. Osip was very taken with Marina. In her memoirs she gives a detailed description of my brother's stay, and prints the verses that he dedicated to her, including one written at about this time, "I kiss her sun-browned elbow and her waxen brow."

In Koktebel Osip and Alexander received a telegram from Father, announcing that Mother was close to death. I had earlier received a telegram from Mother, congratulating me on my entry to the Polytechnical Institute, which had given me great pleasure. But only a few days had passed before I received another telegram, from Father, saying that Mother had suffered a severe stroke. She was only 48. There was no air travel then, and my train journey to St Petersburg took two long days, in complete ignorance of Mother's condition, which was in fact serious. Father was out of his mind with worry: my brothers were still in Koktebel. We put Mother into the Petropavlovsk Hospital, which housed the Women's Medical Institute. She did not regain consciousness, and died three days later. Osip and Alexander arrived literally just in time for the burial.

The break-up of the Mandelstam family dates from Mother's death. We at once felt empty and unsettled. We were tortured by the thought that we were responsible for Mother's early death, for our selfishness and lack of consideration. Mother's death left its mark on the spirit of all her sons, especially on the most impressionable of us, Osip. He dedicated to her the poem "They buried my mother in the shining Temple of the Jews." As Osip grew older, he felt more and more guilty about Mother. As time passed, Osip understood finally how indebted he was to her, what she had done for him. This was apparent especially during the dark days of his exile.

I felt a growing dislike for my father in those early days after Mother's death. I have already written about the strained relationship between my parents. Things had deteriorated during Mother's last years, because another woman had entered Father's life. Since the beginning of the war, Father had rented a small workshop for dressing hides, at Belostrov on the banks of the River Sestra, by the Finnish frontier. This workshop and the adjoining house belonged to the Nielsens, who were immigrants from Sweden. The owner was an old man, but his wife was in the prime of life, "of a Balzacian age" as they say, and she set her sights on Father. He stayed overnight more and more often at Belostrov. I never heard any talk at home about the Nielsens, and do not know how much Mother knew, but the atmosphere was tense.

Father was drawn not only to this woman, but to his work as well. He was an expert dresser of kid-skins and he did all the work himself, only occasionally hiring an extra hand. They made leather jerkins out of the black skins. Such jackets became a sort of uniform after the Revolution for government dignitaries, and they were in great demand. In 1918 the Nielsens returned to Sweden and the workshop was closed.

Although I was the youngest of the three brothers, I could not bear to live with Father after Mother's death. After a few months I left home and moved into a garret, a sort of artist's studio, which a schoolfriend, Vadim Konrady, let me have. Their house on Pesochnaya Street contained a separate apartment of several rooms with an attic on the sixth floor, and this was what they let to me.

In 1917 my maternal grandmother, who had lived with us, also died. This freed Father's hands, and he gave up the lease on our last apartment on Kameno-Ostrovskoye Prospekt, sold the furniture, and rented a room for himself on the Petrograd Side, on Bolshaya Spasskaya Street. He took there the remains of our furniture, the bookcase, the writing table, and a chair with a bow back and arms bearing the inscription "Haste makes waste". Osip, with my help, rented a room near me on Pesochnaya Street, while Alexander moved in with friends. So here I was, living on my own. This move from family life to independence was made easy to me by the warm and friendly help of the Konrady family. I found work comparatively easily with the Petrograd Committee of the Union of Municipalities, on Nevsky Prospekt at No. 72. From its windows I could observe the stormy events of St Petersburg life during the February 1917 Revolution. I saw the crowds on the streets, the Cossacks forcing their way into the demonstrations and beating people with their whips, a police ambush in the Catholic church. Then undercover policeman machine-gunned the mob from the rooftops.

I could not remain a simple observer during those days of ferment. People were being killed out there, they needed help and there was no one to give it. Knowing that a first-aid service had been set up at Warsaw Station, I showed up there almost on the first day and began work. The Union of Municipalities put a decent fleet of hospital vehicles at the disposal of the student contingent — covered wagons with a red cross on the sides. I was elected head of the contingent, and we drew up our regulations (I have them still) for the whole company, and started work at once.

Our team of 20 students accomplished a great deal. We served every one of the city districts, and managed to save the life of more than one wounded man. Even now, 60 years on, it is heartening to know that we started the first-aid service in the city, and that I played my part in it.

While this social conflict was raging, the Kerensky Government was still waging war against the Germans, and fresh drafts were being conscripted into the army all the time. Deferment was granted to university students, but I was called up and became a cadet at the Mikhailovsky Artillery College, which was in Petrograd, near the Finland Station.

Strict traditions still held sway at the Mikhailovsky College, among them the demeaning institution of "fagging", which gave senior cadets the right to lord it over the younger ones. You could be woken up in the night and forced to carry a senior on your shoulders to the lavatory. Their arrogance was boundless. Drill was the most important subject at the College. The aim was to turn civilian youngsters in the shortest possible time into brave, smart cadets, future officers of the Russian Army. For the first month they kept us new recruits literally locked up within the College walls, with only brief visits from relatives. Osip was the first to visit me in those stressful days of isolation. My older brothers were not yet in the armed forces, and were excited by the events of the first months of the February 1917 revolution, with their demonstrations and gatherings, life welling out on to the city streets, and the crowds listening to speakers and agitators from all parties, from the Constitutional Democrats to the Bolsheviks.

Our College was hardly a cloister itself, and passions ran high there too. Even the February Revolution and the policies of the Provisional Government found little favour with most of the staff. There was a clear-cut distinction amongst the political views of the cadets. The majority, more than half, was drawn from the military academies, closed military schools, whose basic task was to train future officers, loyal to the Tsar and fatherland, dedicated to the monarchy.

The remainder had entered the College through call-up, like me, and until then had been students at various universities. With few exceptions, the cadets supported the Provisional Government and were loyal to Kerensky. Among them were many Socialist Revolutionaries and Menshevik Socialist democrats. One group keenly supported the Soviets and the Bolsheviks — it was made up of common soldiers who were lodged separately in Lamansky Lane, near the stables housing the artillery and cavalry horses. Contact between the cadets and the soldiers was sporadic and fortuitous.

During the tense days of General Kornilov's advance on Petrograd, it became known that our batteries would be called to take part in the impending defence of the city and of the Provisional Government. But a conspiracy was afoot in the College. The intention was, on our departure from the city, to shoot all those who sympathised with the Revolution and the Provisional Government and to go over to Kornilov. The conspiracy was uncovered, and the College was withdrawn from any active service.

During our summer encampment at Krasnoye Selo, the Monarchists among the cadets almost did away with the College's few Jews. One night, we were in barracks on the eve of the Jewish Sabbath, with only the duty officer present. With cries of abuse reminiscent of the Black Hundreds, the Monarchists fell upon the sleeping Jews and began to suffocate them with pillows. The duty officer was far away and, if the non-partisan cadets among us had not interfered, nobody would have prevented a terrible outcome of this nocturnal pogrom.

In the autumn the Winter Palace became the headquarters, and later the last stronghold, of the Provisional Government. Here ministers worked without respite and in permanent session under Kerensky's leadership, and here assembled the last army units loyal to him, including one of our batteries.

On 24th October it was our battery's turn to be on duty there. There was chaos inside the Palace, with cadets from the infantry colleges, soldiers from the Women's Shock Troops, various civilians — everyone got mixed up, overflowed the staircases, and filled the main rooms, whose windows overlooked the Palace Square. Here the palace defenders erected a huge barricade in front of the main door built of logs and bristling with machine-guns. The representative of the Provisional Government, the lanky Palchinsky, tried to impose some order on all this chaos, but it was no use by then. The square was surrounded on all sides by a sea of people — soldiers, sailors, Red Guards. Everyone understood that the final assault was about to take place. A deputation set out from the City Duma, headed by the mayor, Isaev. These naive, politically illiterate people tried to enter the square in an attempt at appeasement. They had only reached the Moika when the Red Guards stopped them and told them to return while the going was good.

Our battery's guns were in the Palace's small inner garden. A handful of the Mikhailovsky cadets, forming one battery of six guns, resolutely refused to play any military role. Most of us thought it inconceivable to fire on the people. The chaos, helplessness and disorder shown by the weakness of the authorities already in its death-throes convinced us that this decision was correct.

From the Neva, through the back entrance, the first groups of soldiers from the Pavlovsk Regiment were already forcing their way in. We of the Mikhailovsky College decided to make contact with the Revolutionary War Committee, and negotiate the hand-over of our weapons. I and two companions were appointed for this purpose and led through the Neva gate and the Winter Palace ditch to the nearest barracks. Even now, with tensions at breaking-point on the brink of the assault, they spoke to us without animosity and behaved with absolute trust. They promised to return us all to the College, after disarming us as a precautionary measure and taking our word that we would not involve ourselves in the struggle against the new Soviet government.

The Soviet of People's Commissars decided to demobilize the students and return them to their universities to complete their higher education. So our epaulettes and spurs were removed but we kept our uniforms, civilian dress being almost unobtainable for the moment.

I did not wish to return to the Polytechnical Institute. On the basis of my experience of life at that time I decided that my vocation was different, and chose the most humane of all careers, that of medicine. With considerable pains, and having overcome a number of formal difficulties, I became a medical student at the former Institute of Women's Medicine, now re-named the First Institute of Medicine.

It was not easy to be a student in those years. There were no grants, times were cold and hungry, and what scanty food there was, was rationed. We did whatever we could to earn money: loaded firewood, worked as medical orderlies, or joined factory cooperatives.

The student unions were instrumental in improving our conditions and helping with academic matters, and in keeping us in touch with what was going on outside. The most important of these bodies was the University Soviet of Senior Students. Its main task was to find work for medical students and to improve their material conditions. The students were greatly helped by its canteen, organised with funds from its mutual-aid budget. As well as temporary work for the students, they provided help to those especially in need, organizing recitals of famous writers, poets and musicians. These took place in the huge assembly hall.

The spring of 1918 arrived. A number of students left the Institute in search of a better life. The efforts of the Senior Student Soviet to find work for them, and the help of its mutual fund, were just drops in the ocean. My friends and I had the brilliant idea of forming a market-gardening cooperative, working in the summer holidays on the land, and gathering the produce in the autumn, together with any other meagre earnings of the cooperative, so as to have enough to see us through our winter studies.

We began with the search for a plot of land and housing, the necessary funds, the horses and livestock, the seed, etc. Our choice fell on the old estate of Bely Val, near Luga, and soon the white headscarves of the girl students coloured the meadows, now transformed into cultivated fields, as they tended the young corn shoots.

One fine day Osip turned up at Bely Val and asked to join our cooperative. Many of us knew him as a poet, from his book *Stone*, from his newspaper publications and from his public readings. My companions agreed to help Osip. And thus among the white headscarves of the girls there appeared in the fields the figure of the poet Osip Mandelstam — a dyed-in-the-wool city-dweller totally unsuited in physique and temperament to this sort of work. He lasted three days with difficulty and became terribly tired, until finally, quite worn out, he returned to town.

Translated by James Escomb

Evgeny Mandelstam

The above is an excerpt from the memoirs of Evgeny Mandelstam (1898-1979), the poet's younger brother. The memoirs describe the family's early history, their everyday lives and their complex relationships, family friends and the mileu in which the poet spent his youth. These are all first-hand accounts and are our only source on the poet's early years, before he met his wife Nadezhda, a period least researched in the ample literature available on Mandelstam in all languages. The family's private life is described against the background of turbulent historic events — the First World War, the Revolution and the Civil War in Russia, and this, like any witness accounts, makes it a priceless historical document.

Evgeny Mandelstam was a doctor by profession. He was actively involved in charity work from his days as a medical student. He raised funds for hospitals and also worked in them on a voluntary basis. After the Revolution Evgeny Mandelstam helped organise first-aid medical services in Petrograd. During the 1930s his medical work concentrated on the hygiene of labour. At the outbreak of war he was called upon to serve as an epidemiologist and during those harrowing months of the Leningrad Siege he headed the medical service of the "Road of Life", the only thin thread connecting the besieged city with the mainland.

Evgeny Mandelstam was also involved in some literary activities. Even in his college days he worked for the Leningrad branch of the Moscow society of dramatists and composers, and later he served on the committee of Assistance to Writers. More than ten years of his life were devoted to these activities, and it was this introduction to the literary community that stimulated his own potential for writing. His first literary attempt dates back to the pre-war years when he wrote his first popular-science film scripts. After his demobilisation from the army he continued writing film scripts. This work combined his literary talent with his interest in the sciences. About fifty popular science films were based on his scripts, some even won prizes. His film on genetic engineering ("In the Depth of Living Matter", with N.Zhinkin, and D.Danin, director: M. Kligman) was awarded the State Prize, the Lomonosov Prize and the Badge of Honour at the Montreal World Fair. Evgeny was working on this film during the years of the reactionary Lysenkoism. Despite the support of the scientific community, it took him nine years to get permission to make this film.

This year Evgeny Mandelstam's memoirs will be published in full together with the correspondence of all three Mandelstam brothers, Osip, Alexander and Evgeny, Osip's correspondence with his wife and her correspondence with her father.

Evgeniya Zenkevich

Nadezhda Mandelstam

There is no need to describe here the role of Nadezhda Mandelstam (born 1899 Nadezhda Khazina in Saratov) in the poet's life and subsequent fate of his poetic heritage. Translated into many languages, including English, her books — *Hope Against Hope* and *Hope Abandoned* — are well known around the world.

Anna Akhmatova writes: "Osip's love for his wife was immense, larger than life. When she had an operation in Kiev he stayed at the hospital for several days, sleeping in the watchman's backroom. He wouldn't let her leave his side, wouldn't let her take a job. He was madly jealous. He sought her advice about each line in his verse. I've never seen a more devoted couple. His published letters to Nadezhda completely confirm my impression of them."

After her husband's death she managed to collect and preserve most of his writings. Moreover, she smuggled them to Princeton University in USA, which was a very brave thing to do at the time.

Had Nadezhda Mandelstam been less brave and less loving, Mandelstam would have died several years earlier and his work would almost certainly have perished.

Nadezhda suffered banishment and humiliation, but managed to survive her husband's death by leading an inconspicuous existence as a teacher of English in remote provincial towns. In 1956 she was allowed to come back to Moscow where she wrote her memoirs describing the ordeals she shared with her poet husband.

Her books are written in the manner of "table talks" and her friends remember these stories as she told them. All three books of memoirs are in fact a detailed commentary on the poet's life and work. Many Mandelstam scholars noted a strong element of bias in her books and occasionally an opinionated tone, something only to be expected from a woman completely dedicated to the memory of her beloved husband.

She had a considerable talent for self-expression and was described by Joseph Brodsky as one of the outstanding writers of her day.

Nadezhda Volpin

Reminiscences of Mandelstam and his Wife

Man and Wife

Where and when was it? Most probably at my apartment on Vassilievsky Island in 1925. Osip Mandelstam came with his wife, Nadezhda Khazina. She had previously been a painter but all this was in the past, although sometimes she would suddenly remember and reproach her husband, to whom she was utterly devoted, saying, "You have killed the painter in me!" And he would reply, "How can you possibly kill an artist? If an artist lets himself be killed, then he was never any sort of artist!"

A look of profound resentment clouded his wife's face, yet it was also a look of humility.

Nadezhda's Skirt

Osip Mandelstam and his wife Nadezhda were spending the winter in Tsarskoe Selo, living in two enormous salons — you could scarcely call them rooms — in one of the palaces. Firewood was needed to heat them and all of Mandelstam's hard-earned income from translation and editorial work went into logs for the fire, then straight up the chimney. A cart-load of wood was gone within a week. When the poet and his wife came to Leningrad for a day or two on business, the wide sofa in my room on Thirteenth Street was pressed into service for an overnight stay. I had only two rooms. The nurse-maid and my son lived in the larger one, which measured some thirty square metres. The smaller room served as my bedroom and study. Osip and Nadezhda would arrive and make themselves at home in my apartment. Occasionally they took me out to Tsarskoe Selo, to their spartan home. They probably had much more money than me or most of my friends, but they lived a shabby, disorganized existence.

Pointing to me, Osip said to his wife: "Look, dear, at her, she has a nice skirt, she has a nice blouse! Why don't you have anything?"

Nadezhda Mandelstam straightened her lopsided, grey rag of a skirt, with its uneven hem, held together with safety-pins (alas, it was her only one just like mine), she snapped back at him, angry at his reproach.

Matteo Falcone

This is how they used to walk together, the Poet and his wife, along Nevsky Prospekt, Liteiny Prospekt, along my Thirteenth Street. Osip strode ahead, erect, his head and shoulders thrown back, arms akimbo. Nadezhda, short, long-nosed, rosy-cheeked, always lagged a little behind, and every now and again, with rapid short steps, she hurried along to catch up with him. She carried his briefcase — "He can't carry it himself, it's his heart..." So with her heavy load, the obedient wife would follow behind her Matteo Falcone, for it was not fitting for the Corsican to carry anything but his rifle.

I am the Ode!

Once, after a long interval, Osip and Nadezhda came to see me. My little boy, who was two at the time, was lying on his cot. The poet leaned down over him:

"Do you know who I am?"

"Yes."

"You're lying. What's my name?"

"You're Uncle O.!"

Mandelstam burst into a joyful laugh.

"True! True! That's "O" for Ode. That's my hallmark. I am the Ode!"

The "Leningrad Press" is Paying Today

Mandelstam and his wife were again staying overnight on my sofa. In the morning, his eyes scarcely open, Osip remembered:

"The Leningrad Press is paying today. We should go along. Have you any business there?"

"Unfortunately they don't owe me anything. But there's no harm in dropping in on Marshak... Do you have anything to get there?"

"Not a thing. But it's a good time to request a loan from someone."

We had breakfast and off we went. Slowly we made our way up the stairs and encountered a thin, middle-aged lady, very preoccupied with something. Mandelstam ran up to her as if she were his dearest friend.

"Olga Dmitrievna! I congratulate you with all my heart! Is your book still being typeset, or is it already published?"

"It's published! I got my first payment today."

The book was Olga Forsh's "Dressed in Stone" about prisoners in the Schlisselburg.

Politely, Mandelstam broached the subject of a loan. The happy author interrupted him in mid-stream:

"Osip, I really do understand, really, for heaven's sake!"

Olga Forsh drew an old, worn wallet from her handbag, and opened it before her petitioner. A fat wad of high-denomination banknotes bulged from it.

"Help yourself, my friend! Take whatever you need! I'm so happy that I don't have to ask for any more loans myself but can give and give!"

Her eyes shone.

Mandelstam calmly took a few notes and, without counting them, thrust them into his breast pocket. For politeness' sake, he said the conventional...

"I'll pay you back in a few days..."

And, courteously taking his leave, he went on his way.

They both knew that he would "forget" to repay the loan. That was understood by both lender and borrower.

I'd Like an Advance

This I remember from an even earlier time.

The KUBU had just been formed. Its rules had been announced. The KUBU took under its wing a small group of writers, Mandelstam amongst them. The rules were read aloud before the future wards of KUBU who had assembled. Osip Mandelstam put forward a request: could they advance him the money for his funeral expenses (such an allowance was included in the rules). He offered his written promise that his family would not apply a second time for this aid.

Years passed. His family never requested the money. Nobody knows now where the poet's body is buried, or even if it was ever buried. Was the advance granted? Some say it was. The KUBU board had enough sense of humour to comply with such an unusual request. Did they understand that everyone possible had to help him in his hopelessly disorganized life? Any other poet compared to Osip Mandelstam was like a spider weaving its web compared to a silkworm. Georgy Shengeli could render twenty stanzas of Byron's "Don Juan" into Russian in twenty four hours, while it took Mandelstam three entire weeks to translate a single Petrarch sonnet. Is there even one line in all his poetry that is not inspired? One line in all his prose that is not weighty? Therefore, everyone who was at all concerned with poetry had the responsibility to look after and to cherish this marvel of a poet!

Translated by James Escomb

Nadezhda Volpin was born 1900 in Mogilev-on-Dnieper. In 1903, her family moved to Moscow where Nadezhda finished grammar school. In 1919, as an author of a considerable number of verses, although unpublished, she is accepted into the Poets' Union. However, this does not help her get her poems published except one or two in the Poets' Union's collections. She becomes a professional translator. In 1919 she met Sergei Esenin with whom she became very close. Recently she published her memoirs about Sergei Esenin. The stories about Mandelstam and his wife are part of her memoirs.

Mandelstam in English

Complete Poetry, tr. Burton Ruffel and Alla Burago, introduction by Sidney Monas, State University of New York Press, Albany, 1973.

Osip Mandelstam, *Stone,* tr. by Robert Tracy, Harvill, 1991.

Mandelstam. The Collected Critical Prose and Letters, tr. Jane Gary Harris and Constance Link, Ardis, Ann Arbor, 1979; Harvill, 1991.

The Prose of Osip Mandelstam, tr. Clarence Brown, Princeton University Press, 1965.

Talking about Dante, tr. Clarence Brown and Robert Hughes, Oklahoma, 1965.

Clarence Brown, *Mandelstam*, Cambridge University Press, 1976.

The Moscow Notebook, tr. Richard McKane, Bloodaxe Books, 1992.

Omry Ronen, *An Approach to Mandelstam*, Jerusalem, 1983.

Nadezhda Mandelstam, *Hope Against Hope*, *Hope Abandoned*, Collins Harvill, London, and Atheneum, New York, 1974 .

Grigory Freidin, *A Coat of Many Colours: Osip Mandelstam and his mythology of Self-presentation*, University of California Press, Berkeley, Los Angeles, London, 1987.